To Debora

Ila's Diamonds

Donna Banks (signature)

by

Donna M. Banks

Thank you for your support (handwritten)

author**HOUSE**®

AuthorHouse™
1663 Liberty Drive, Suite 200
Bloomington, IN 47403
www.authorhouse.com
Phone: 1-800-839-8640

First published by AuthorHouse   3/26/2008

ISBN: 978-1-4343-5252-1 (sc)

Library of Congress Control Number: 2008902035

Printed in the United States of America
Bloomington, Indiana

This book is printed on acid-free paper.

Dedication

To my mother, Lorraine, who has been my biggest fan all of my life, I believe I have done and said all the things she would have loved to have said and done. She is a wonderful mother and was a dedicated wife to my father for fifty years.

To my dad, Jackson, I miss you every minute, every hour of every day.

To my sister, Christine, whom I love very much. The most generous person I know.

To my nephew, Gary, I hope love will bring us back together.

To my brother, Gilbert—lost in a life of substance abuse and one of the smartest men I know.

To my brother, Jack—a quiet storm, a virtuous man, and a man with a clear understanding about what he wants and how to obtain it. I marvel that we were born into the same family.

To my best friend, Sharon Dooley Ponton…girl, we are connected in so many ways. Your spirit wraps around my heart. I thank God for your friendship.

To my niece, Tomika Freeman—you are the daughter I should have had.

To my goddaughters, Alicia and Stacey—you are bold and strong. I am so impressed with both of you.

To Ree Ree, my mirror image.

To Gerald Chester, thank you for the parachute.

To all the men who have been in my life thank you for the lessons.

To my son, Gregory—when I breathe, I feel you. You are my essence; I love the man you have become in spite of me and all of my hang-ups.

To my grandmother, Sarah, who made sure I was grounded in the Word of God and whose prayers have kept me.

To my husband, Robert—the man who made me whole. I love you more each day.

To my Girl Friends For Life (GFFLs)

To everyone in Homewood in Pittsburgh, Pennsylvania.

It was 1976 and I didn't realize that a napkin could serve so many purposes in the business world. It is used to keep the condensation on a glass from damaging a countertop or table. It is used to wipe your mouth, and for professional men to write their thoughts about what they can or cannot do for you.

Standing next to the four-star general at a reception for the Star Wars project that had just been completed for the Pentagon, I thought my world could not get any better. I was the only Black person in the room, but that was not unusual for me. I had learned to blend in as much as possible in these situations and had become the staple (or token) on so many occasions. It didn't faze me any longer. However, at this reception I received the napkin. It was a purple cocktail napkin with the words, "What Can I Do For You?" written on it. I was shocked, looked at the individual who had handed it to me with the RCA dog look, and walked away. I placed the napkin in my purse and moved on to another area of the reception to contemplate what to do with the purple cocktail napkin in my purse.

I returned that night to the apartment I shared with my brother on "G" Street South West in Washington, DC. His substance abuse had become destructive and he was increasingly hard to be around. As I walked through the door, Sidney, his girlfriend at the moment, Rob the banker, Sinclair the waste management supervisor, and my brother, was sitting about the table telling lies, drinking beer, and doing lines of heroin. This camaraderie went on for about forty minutes, and then it became very quiet as they all went into that incredible nod. Since it was an efficiency apartment, my bed was in what should have been the small living room. As I showered and changed for bed in the midst of nodding people, I knew that moving would have to be placed into high gear. As I lay down for the night, I had become accustomed to sleeping with people all around who were doing whatever. As night turned into dawn, people began to leave, and I was glad to have at least two hours of sleep with no one in the room with me. I heard the door close and felt sweet relief that I was hopefully alone. As I dosed off, I felt the covers on the other side of the bed lift. Rob, the banker, thought that sharing my bed would suit him in his haze. I turned over, asked him to get out of the bed, and screamed for my brother. Unfortunately, for me, he had left with Sidney and Sinclair. I was alone with Rob. I knew that fighting him was not the answer. Knowing his condition once he shot his load, he would be asleep for a while. Silently, he entered me from the back, came, and fell asleep. Moving was paramount now. I never told my brother about that night. In the next week, I moved to a small apartment complex in Arlington, Virginia.

The complex was on a dead end street (Perfect). It was within walking distance to a dry cleaner, *Publixs*, a small drug store, and I66 was soon to be right along the route. No one wanted to live there because of all the construction on I66. It was a perfect and safe haven for me. No one could just be in the area, just happen to drop by, or be in the neighborhood. After living in an apartment that was like a *7-Eleven* (open all night), this was going to be like living in a luxury hotel. Plus, it was one block to the metro and then two metro stops to work. It was a perfect location. I was on the second floor, and had one bedroom, a kitchen, and a small living room/ dining room connection.

The apartment had absolutely no closet space. It had wall units for heating and air conditioning along with prehistoric roaches, but it was mine and it only cost $225.00 per month plus electric. I didn't know then that it was the "plus electric" that would keep me broke most of the time.

My father and his friend, Eddie, brought me what they could from my hometown in Pittsburgh. I slept on a mattress on the floor for many months, but it was well worth it. I painted, bombed the roaches, cleaned the hardwood floors, placed a small dinette in the room connected to the living room, and called it home.

Getting to know the new neighborhood was great fun. I liked walking into all the small mom and pop stores that were still very prevalent during that time and getting to know everyone on a first-name basis. I even found a furniture store that I could lay-away items and pay biweekly for furniture with no finance charges—just a handshake and a promise. I thought it was great luck, but as I look back, I now know that God's hand had been stretched out to me. The prayers from my mother and grandmother were surrounding my very being, but to me it was just great luck. Boy, was I wrong.

I had been so involved with the move and working long hours, I had completely forgotten about the purple napkin until I was about to go to a jazz club off Constitution Avenue. I thought a small purse would be in order. As I opened the purse to place my compact, lipstick, keys and money inside, there was the napkin with the words, "What Can I Do For You?" written on it. The message was still fresh and not smudged. I decided that I would get a napkin and write my response to him. At the appropriate time, I would place it in his hand.

It took me two weeks and a package of napkins later, to write my response, "What Do You Believe You Could Do For Me?" Okay, now all I had to do was place it in his hand. He was a consultant and not present on my job daily. He came

3

around only once a month, turned in his reports, attended numerous meetings, and returned home to Phoenix. I knew his travel plans because I had been making them for him for at least two years. I never thought he would approach me. He would say things on the phone, like "Hi, beautiful," or "I can't get a ride. Pick me up from the airport." Of course, I would reply with either, "I have a driver for you," or "I made a car reservation for you already," and then I would laugh. Now I see he was trying to take it to the next step. My opportunity came on a Monday morning. He arrived around 10:00 a.m. I gave him his meeting schedule and the napkin. He reviewed his schedule, looked at the napkin, laughed, and walked away.

The day went by with little fanfare and just as I was ready to leave the telephone rang. I picked up the receiver.

He said, "I can pay your rent, your car note, and place money in your personal account. But, you can't have others (men) around while I am in town." I paused and said, "I'll get back to you." I hung up the phone, and looked around the office, because I knew my face was turning red—or as red as a lady of my complexion could turn. He returned to Phoenix after a one-week business trip to Washington and I had not given him an answer.

In the meantime, I had met Mr. Right—Rodney, who was a fine secret service agent, tall, dark, not so handsome, but looked stunning in a black suit. He seemed to be at every corner of my job. Looking, whispering into his wrist and he always had a smile that could make you believe that his teeth might not be real. For about a month, we played the game of, "Good morning, how are you? What a nice day. How was your weekend? Finally, on a cold Washington morning, he was leaving the building as I was entering. I did my normal pleasantry

Then he said, "Meet me for a drink."

"Where?" I asked."

"The Waterside Inn in South West at 7:00 p.m.," he replied.

I said, "Okay."

Of course, it turned out to be one of my busiest days. My boss was in Europe and calling every hour to have certain papers faxed, or sent via Federal Express. Or, he wanted me to read messages to him over the phone. And, it was his wife's birthday. Of course, I waited until the last minute to order the roses and to pick up her Christian Dior scarf and I hand delivered everything to the upper northwest.

As the day progressed, I knew that 7:00 p.m. would not be a reasonable time for me to get from Alexandria, Virginia to the upper northwest, and then arrive in South West by 7:00 p.m. To add to my dilemma, there were no cell phones back then. I did the next best thing. I called the Waterside Inn and asked the bartender to look for Rodney. I told him to send Rodney two drinks and give him my apology that I was running late. Fortunately, the Inn was not very crowded that night. He found Rodney, explained my situation, and served him his two drinks. I arrived at 7:30 p.m. By the time I got there, another lady had joined him at his table. That kind of thing seemed to happen to me more often than not. Dating in a city where the women clearly out numbered the men, a woman really had to have confidence in herself and an ability to charm almost anyone. I walked over to the table, and introduced myself to the young lady. I asked her what she was drinking. I walked to the bar, introduced myself to the bartender, tipped him for helping me out, bought her the drink, and walked back to the table. I gave her the drink. Then I requested that she find somewhere else to sit. It worked that time, but there have been times when it didn't work so well. She left with her drink, and I took a seat across from Rodney.

A very nice jazz combo was playing, and the Inn was filling up. The drinks were flowing. I was drinking Hennessy straight up with a water back. Rodney was drinking Grey Goose with orange and cranberry juice. I believe that his intention was to get me drunk and take advantage of me. He didn't know that I came from a family who believed in starting their day with a shot and a beer was like breakfast. Around 11:00 p.m., I drove Rodney home.

When I got back home, my neighbors, Paula and Drew, were on the prowl for weed and beer. They heard me enter the apartment building and were waiting for me at the top of the stairs. I knew what they wanted. We had that non-verbal communication going on because the building was full of police officers and other government types. I gave them two rolling rocks and two joints. They were quite happy. I soon heard wild laughter, moaning and then silence. I stayed up reading Jonathan Kellerman and wondered how I was going to face Rodney in the morning.

As luck would have it, Rodney was deployed to another building, so I didn't have to look at him or exchange greetings. It was payday and of course the entire office was in a good mood. The day went by fast and by 5:15 p.m. the office was empty. I usually stayed until 6:00 p.m. because my boss was always traveling in different time zones. If I stayed a little later, we would get a chance to talk about what he might need the next day, or if he wanted to change his travel plans or whatever. The phone rang at about 5:45 p.m. and it was Phoenix.

"Hi, I'm coming into town on the 15th and wondered if I could stay at your place."

I was speechless.

Then he said, "Have you looked in your lower left-hand drawer today?"

I said, "No!"

He said, "Take a look."

I opened the drawer and there was an envelope marked, "Open me." I opened the envelope. Inside was an ATM card and a pin number.

I picked the phone back up and he said, "Are you there?"

I said, "Yes."

He said, "My plane arrives on the 15th at 8:00 p.m., Washington National Airport. Please don't be late."

Before I could answer, I heard the dial tone. Oh, shit! What do I do now? How did he put that in my desk?

It seemed like the 15th would never get here. Finally, the day arrived. I was dressed in a red suit, red shoes, and a sheer black blouse. I stayed at the office until 6:00 p.m. Then, I immediately went to Washington National Airport. I was much too eager. I got there in twenty minutes and had to keep circling. At 8:25 p.m. I saw him come out the door. I drove up. He got inside, handed me a small package, and told me it was from Brussels. As we drove back to my apartment, few words were spoken. I just didn't know what to say and I hoped that Paula and Drew were not standing outside, or waiting for me inside.

As we entered my apartment, I suddenly felt how meager it must look to him. I felt sure that since he was accustomed to staying in four and five star hotels, this small tenement would not be to his liking.

Boy, was I wrong. He became comfortable very fast. He took his small travel bag straight into the bedroom, pulled out a bottle of Absolut, a plastic bag with a white substance in it, and a bottle of Bayer aspirins. He asked me to bring him two glasses with ice. Then he said he was going to take a shower. I was still motionless at the front door. I said things like, "Oh, okay. Anything else?"

By that time, he was in the shower. I got the glasses, the ice, and a tray of cheese and crackers. He strutted from the bathroom with the towel around his neck, and I was very surprised at his size. I had always been told that Caucasian men were very small. However, he was the exception. He sat on the side of the bed, made himself a drink, and requested that I go take a shower. He really didn't like perfume and wanted me to smell only of soap. I was compliant. I walked to the front door; double locked it, and went quickly to the shower. It seemed as if I was in the shower for a very long time, but once I arrived back in the bedroom, it had only been ten minutes. He had dimmed the lights, had put Etta James on the record player, and was in the bed. My feet went cold. I backed up, walked to the kitchen, got myself a rolling rock, drank most of it with one gulp, and returned to the bedroom, with my rolling rock in hand.

He said, "Please, join me."

At this point, he had taken the saucer that I had the cheese on, and wiped it off. Then I saw the white substance. He had rolled a dollar bill very tight and the white powder had been placed in rows. Okay, I was not completely naïve. I knew it was cocaine, but I certainly had no idea how to use the substance. He sniffed a line and handed me the dollar bill. I finished the rolling rock and sniffed a line the same way he had. I thought my head would fall off. All of a sudden, my nose began to run and I wanted to jump up and dance to Etta James. However, I controlled myself. He did another line, handed me the dollar bill again, and I sniffed another line. I felt numb. He drank his Absolut on ice and reached over to cup my breast. I recoiled. He was bothered. He requested that I lay down. He placed the plate of cocaine on the snack table, and demanded that I open my legs. I did, and then he took the remaining row and sprinkled it on my trimmed pussy. He had oral sex for approximately twenty minutes and that's when I lost my mind. It was my first oral sex experience. The last thing I remembered was Etta James' "At Last" skipping in the tracks. I woke up at 4:00 a.m., took the needle off of Etta James, and turned off the record player. I set the clock for 7:00 a.m., and went back to bed.

The next morning, he straightened up, took a shower, had coffee, two pieces of toast, and two Bayer aspirins. He took a cab to work. I took the subway. It was a blissful two weeks. Every night we went to a different restaurant—La Petite Mansion, Lion Doir, Ethiopian and Jamaican restaurants. He loved good exotic food.

For two years, this relationship was more than perfect. I could see whomever I wanted, and do whatever I wanted to do while he was out of town. When he was in town, he wanted my undivided attention. No problem!

He was an avid reader, and he loved to read out loud to me. He would always begin with Homer, move on to John Steinbeck, and end with small passages from Plato and the life and times of Henry the Eighth. Of course, I had never been exposed to this literature. I believe I read Henry the Eighth in high school, but when we moved to a predominantly white neighborhood when I was fourteen, I was introduced to Quaaludes, grass that was laced with black beauties, and window pane acid. So, I don't remember a lot of my high school years, but, I digress.

A world of art museums, plays at the Ford Theater, The Kennedy Center, and venturing through the Air and Space Museum was opened up to me through this relationship. Eating mussels, clams, oysters on the half shell, and anything in a white cream sauce, were all foreign to me until now. This was the best education a young lady from Homewood—a small town in Pittsburgh, Pennsylvania—could wish for and receive.

I didn't know much about his life outside of our relationship. I knew he had two children and a devoted wife. There were times when I wanted to know more. I know that he lived in a lavish house, with a pool, and a detached house where his parents lived. It was worlds away from where we stayed in Arlington, Virginia. I often wondered why a man like him would want to spend time in a small, one-bedroom apartment where the air and heat came from a wall unit.

It was getting harder to hide the relationship at work. He was becoming very bold. As I look back, I believe that he told some of his buddies about our relationship.

The general's daughter came to me one day and asked, "When you turn in Phoenix's travel expense report, there aren't any hotel receipts. Where do you think he is staying?"

I said, "He always tells me he is staying with friends, and all he requires is gratuitous subsistence. I wouldn't question him about what he turns in or does not turn in."

She said, "I think he's dating the accountant in the grants department."

"Perhaps," I said. "But I wouldn't know. He is a very private man. I try to respect that."

Getting no information from me, she said, "Okay, I've got to go."

I hoped I had not given her any idea that it was me, but, of course, she wouldn't think it was me. I was not white man skinny and there was no way a man of his caliber would be with an administrative assistant, let alone a Black administrative assistant. With that, the phone rang.

"Hi" he said. "Come to my office. I need to make reservations for a trip to Paris."

I replied, "I'm on my way."

I placed the phone on forward to the receptionist, and walked to his office. I knocked on the door and went in. He requested that I lock the door. I did.

He said, "Lift your skirt and pull down your panties."

I did. He walked over, and demanded that I sit on the edge of the chair. I did. He bent down, and began to eat my pussy like a dog laps up water. That went on for ten minutes, with me practically biting my arm off, knowing I couldn't scream. Once he had his fill, he went into his private bathroom, brushed his teeth, brought me a towel, sat in his chair, and began giving me his itinerary for Paris. I was still catching my breath. The memory still makes my knees weak.

After gaining my composure, I took down his itinerary and left his office. I knew that in three more hours, I would get more of the same. The hours ticked by very slowly. I had a great deal of work to do, so it kept my mind occupied. He was leaving for Paris the very next morning on the red eye and he would be gone for a month. I knew he had plans to go to Paris; I just didn't know when. He never really gave me advance notice. I believe he didn't want me to have time to make plans. Finally, at 6:00 p.m., I removed my heels and changed into tennis shoes to make the walk to the metro. As I walked toward the elevators, my boss called me back to say he had an emergency and needed to complete the white paper we were working on tonight. It needed to go out *Federal Express* to Canada first thing in the morning. Phoenix had left at least an hour before, so I knew he had stopped at *Publix*, picked up dinner, and was preparing it at this very moment. I walked back to my desk, called my apartment, but he didn't answer. I called again. He didn't answer. Finally, on the third call, he answered.

"Hello I figured it was you because it was ringing so insistently."

"Yes," I said. "I have to stay and finish a white paper. Have you started dinner?"

"Not yet. I'll shower, read the paper, and wait for you to come home."

I didn't have the heart to tell him that it would probably take awhile.

I said, "Great, see you soon."

Four hours later, at 10:00 p.m., of course, he was packing. He had left dinner on the stove and a glass of wine on the small dining room table. I could not believe that he would be gone for a month, and this was how it was going to be. He called the driver and sat on the sofa to wait. The car would arrive in fifteen minutes. Of course, he understood, because we chose our jobs. Sometimes having a social life is hard when you're working for the government. We talked about the position I had applied for which would be working with a four star general, and how he had given me a great recommendation. The job was probably in the bag. I thanked him but reminded myself that I was not white, male, skinny, blonde, or connected. There came the dreadful knock on the door. It was the driver. He picked up his suitcase and asked me to grab my sweater and take a ride to the airport with him. Of course, I ran to get my sweater and couldn't wait to spend twenty more minutes with him. As I entered the car, I saw a stack of envelopes on the seat. Each was numbered from one to thirty.

He said, "I have given you an envelope for every day that I will be gone. You can open the first envelope tomorrow morning."

Apparently, I didn't appear excited enough for him.

He said, "What's wrong?"

I said, "A month is a very long time."

He said, "You know what? As soon as I get back, we will take that trip to Williamsburg. I know I've been promising to take you there. But, you do understand that I must go to Phoenix for at least a week before I come back to DC. I must check in on my family."

Of course, I knew that.

He said, "Make the reservations for the Columbus Day weekend, and off we'll go."

By this time, we had arrived at Washington National Airport. He was getting out of the car and my heart left with him.

The ride back to Arlington seemed like hours. I thanked the driver, and walked slowly up the steps. I found Paula and Drew in the heat of an argument and the police were on their way. Just another day in the neighborhood.

I filled the next five weeks with work, happy hours at the Fox Trapp, and with friends. I had joined a woman's organization whose sole purpose was to give scholarships to students at the University of the District of Columbia (UDC). It was a small university at the time, with a minority student enrollment of 80 percent. It was a great group of ladies. I was the youngest at the time and had been put in my place on several occasions. However, it was well worth the education I received from those seasoned veterans. Some had walked with Dr. Martin Luther King. Some had been at the first march on Washington. Some had stories of pickin' cotton and eating pig's feet from a jar. They were fascinating. Most were married to Pullman or metro workers, who had stayed with their jobs and made significant lives for them and their families. The women were also professional teachers, lawyers, and administrators. I had been with the group for four years as the secretary when the president appointed me as the mistress of ceremonies at their annual fashion show/ scholarship benefit at the downtown Hilton. She reiterated that this was what I had been waiting for and now was the time. I was a little apprehensive because our honored guest was Ms. Condoleeza Rice. We were honoring her with our community service award and even then, we knew she was going to be someone special. Little did we know that she would walk with heads of states twenty years later. Putting together the benefit took a collaborative effort. The Hilton sat 1,500 people and all eyes would be on the grand dais and the mistress of ceremonies.

I worked diligently on the benefit, and made sure ticket sales were going as expected. I went to food tastings at the Hilton to help choose the menu items. I contacted entertainment groups, and a troop of fashion icons, at that time "King and I Productions." They always put on a fantastic show, which included the latest fashions, music, and of course, they always had a special guest. Selling tickets or anything else was not my forte. Even as a Girl Scout, I would barter with other Girl Scouts to get my cookie sales done, by doing their homework, or chores at their house. I'd do anything not to have to sell cookies. Through those collaborative efforts, my cookie sales were always high. However, for the benefit, I had to buy my tickets and give them away. Somewhere I had lost my spirit of bartering. I didn't mind because being on that dais was all that mattered.

I managed to open an envelope everyday. The one thing about Phoenix, he was not going to let me squander his money away. The first envelope contained the payment for my light bill for thirty days. The second envelope contained the payment for my car. The third envelope contained the payment for my rent. The fourth envelope was a metro pass for thirty days. The fifth envelope was a gas card. The sixth envelope was a gift certificate to our favorite Chinese restaurant, and so on.

The benefit went off without a hitch, and was very successful. I was totally relaxed on the dais. I felt that I should have been there a long time ago. I felt right at home. The only problem with doing it right the first time was I got a chance to do it on several other occasions after that.

After the benefit time seemed to drag. Phoenix was not due back for another week and my period had not arrived. It was daunting. I could not be pregnant. That, I was sure would ruin everything. The over-the-counter tests were not exact back then. You could only go to your private physician or to the health department. I waited another day or so and then made an appointment at a local clinic. The rabbit died! Okay, do not panic. Make an appointment at the clinic to get rid of the baby and that will be that. Do not tell Phoenix. His religion might get in the way of having an abortion. He was coming home in the next few days. I planned to just wait until he went traveling again, and then I would have the abortion. Oh, but he was very perceptive. He knew when my period was coming by the size of my nipples, or the swell of my ankles and fingers. He even knew just by the roundness of my middle. I believe he kept track of my period by placing a period in his pocket calendar on the day I started. Very cleaver, now that I think back, just to digress a minute, my mother used to count the Kotex. How smart is that? Too funny!

I couldn't wait to see him. I had put on my best leather outfit from Georgetown Leather design, my boots, see-through blouse, and Aromatics Elixir. I was ready to see my man. He was not coming in until 3:30 p.m. I went into work early so that I could leave early. It was a wonderful day in the metropolitan area—nice, crisp, and full of visitors from all over the world. I entered the elevator, showed my ID badge, and began the long elevator ride to the tenth floor. Yes, not that long, but when you are in your first trimester and on an elevator in the early morning, throwing up sounds like an excellent idea. Finally, on the tenth floor, I rounded the corner to my area, and saw everyone huddling together. Some of the ladies were crying. I thought I was not even going to deal with the drama. My man was coming home and nothing was going to bring me down. I began opening my safe and making preparations for the day when one of my co-workers came to my desk. Her eyes were bloodshot and her Kleenex was balled in her hand, as if she had been crying for quite awhile.

"What's wrong?" I asked.

She said, "Phoenix is dead. He died on the slopes in Paris. He had a heart attack. The general wants you to make arrangements to bring the body back to the U.S."

"Me?" I said. "Why Me?"

She replied, "You're really out of it this morning. Haven't you heard?"

"Heard what?" I asked.

"Your promotion came through this morning. You work for the four star general now."

Already my feet had gone cold after hearing that Phoenix was dead. The promotion put me into a catatonic state.

"Thank you" I said to my co-worker. "I'll go see the general now and get directions."

I went to the elevator, took it to the lobby, went into the lobby ladies room, and fell apart.

After about an hour, I returned to my area, called the general on the intercom to thank him for the promotion, and asked how he wanted the transport to take place. I also asked him if I should notify Phoenix's family. He said he would contact the family. All he wanted was to make sure the body got back to the United States with little fanfare. For the rest of the day, I worked on getting Phoenix's body from Paris to the United States, and then on home to Phoenix. I had several conversations with his wife that day, and felt her hurt through the phone. We cried together for a man I loved and a man she adored. I would learn later that Phoenix had a heart condition and that is why he took Bayer aspirin after breakfast all the time.

After an exhausting day, I took the metro home, entered my apartment, went to the kitchen, took down three shots of Hennessy, and crawled into bed. I stayed there for the next forty-eight hours in my Georgetown leather design suit and the baby in my belly. My period of living under grace was over and one of Ila's diamonds was gone.

I opened the last envelope and there were six checks in that envelope to take care of my expenses for the next two months. Somehow, I think he knew he wouldn't be back. Of course, since he was paying most of my bills, I did what every young lady would do. I didn't save any money, and I bought clothes, jewelry, shoes and furniture. My savings account was pitiful and my checking account was worse.

Nevertheless, Phoenix had given me the gift of time to get myself together financially. I miss him everyday. There is an ache in my stomach that won't go away. Oh Yea, I forgot, I am still pregnant. Too funny! That would account for the ache in my stomach.

Four weeks after Phoenix died, I decided to have an abortion. It was a very hard decision. I knew the decision had to be made before I entered by third trimester. After a woman's third trimester, it was against the law to have an abortion except if the mother's life was in danger. I finally began getting rid of his items and all the brochures to Williamsburg. That's when I decided to go to the clinic—the Friday before the Columbus Day holiday—the holiday we were supposed to be in Williamsburg. The deed would be done. I called the clinic, got a 9:00 a.m. appointment, and exhaled.

The clinic was in southwest Washington DC and looked very inviting, until I saw the protestors around the perimeter. They had signs and they seemed to be praying. I didn't look at them. I just bowed my head and entered the clinic. The room was small and almost all the chairs were taken. I entered, signed in and waited for the nurse to call my name. I gazed out the crack in the window. All the windows had blinds on them and were tinted. This was so you could see out, but no one could see in. A sense of finality had come over me. I had gotten used to talking to this baby. I had even given it a name, Jonathan. What was I thinking? Did I really believe that Phoenix would leave his wife and children to be with his concubine and bastard child? I must admit it was nice fantasizing about a big house in Chevy Chase, Maryland; not having to work; and sitting on the big porch. Jonathan and I would be there waiting for Phoenix to get off the metro. Every time I would think those thoughts, I would splash a full glass of water into my face. Since his death, and after learning that Phoenix had a bad heart, I learned the reason he took the Bayer aspirin was to thin his blood. I also learned he was a life long Mormon. I'm sure his parents were turning over in their graves to think that their Mormon son had gotten a Black woman pregnant. Be that as it may, I missed him terribly and was carrying his child. Being pregnant for such a short time has been my pleasure. The room was clearing out. I wondered if they stopped taking appointments at a certain time of day. It was about 10:00 a.m. and I was still sitting in the waiting room.

My mind wandered to when I was in this same situation about five years prior. I was staying with my parents and dating this goofy guy, Paul. Goofy, yes, but loaded. He was an engineer for Westinghouse Electric in Pittsburgh, Pennsylvania, and he had invented a widget for the washer and dryer, which made it run more efficiently. After receiving a patent on the widget, he sold it to Westinghouse Electric and received a large sum of money. He'd continue to receive money, I believe, for the rest of his life. Looking back, Paul's living situation was like the *Psycho* movie. He and his mother lived in a huge house in a section of Pittsburgh called Blackridge. It was a section where Blacks were not allowed to live for many years. But, Paul and his family were light bright, damn near, so they were allowed access to the other side. Me, being dishwater brown, I was only allowed to come in and out of the neighborhood with him on his motorcycle with a helmet on at all times. I don't think his neighbors ever really saw me, or I was the pink elephant in the room that no one said was there. He lavished me with gifts. He was generous with his time, and we made love in his mother's house, while you could hear her rocker going back and forth on the first floor. Very strange. Paul also had an addiction to porn. Between the porn music score, his mother's squeaky chair, and my heavy breathing, it was music to our ears.

We were returning from a day of riding when Paul decided to make a right turn into a small motel in

Monroeville, Pennsylvania. I was unprepared for this stop as I used a diaphragm for birth control and it was not in. It was at home in my purse. I told him I was unprotected.

Of course, he said, "I have all the control, and I will pull out."

That was the day I got pregnant. As I stood at the sink at my mother's house some weeks later, she asked me if I had a problem, and if I needed to talk about it. I said no, that I had it under control. It was years later before I found out she was counting Kotex. Two weeks later, I aborted my first child, Edward. The first of Ila's diamonds was gone on a warm summer day in May.

I named that baby Edward after the love of my life. He was the young man I met in middle school and loved right through high school and into my first year of college. Edward and I dated off and on over five years. One night he walked from his home on the outskirts of Pittsburgh, to my house in six inches of snow. I thought only someone who truly loves me would do that. We spent a great evening—kissing and going to the very limit that all young people go to without really having sex. At midnight, he had to leave. He put on three layers of clothes and walked home in the cold. I thought my heart would beat through my chest when he left. I asked him to call me as soon as he arrived home. Approximately one-and-one-half hours later, he did. We talked all night. I awakened in the morning with the phone in my hand, with the operator's recording asking me to hang up.

My friend, Charmaine, and I would walk ten blocks to watch him and his friend play basketball. You know that is the kind of love you will only have once in your lifetime. Edward loved to go anywhere. We would take the 98 Frankstown bus and ride into downtown Pittsburgh. We'd stay all day, go shopping, eat, and hang out at Point State Park. It was a natural love. We held hands all the time and never went long without touching each other. (Think back.

Can you remember those days? Those were the days with your first love.) I was well into my junior year in high school and Edward was a senior when it was clear that he was gay. We never had sex, but I thought that was because he wanted to wait until we got married.

It was a balmy spring night and we were on our way to the Fantastic Plastic, a new disco located in the Hill district of Pittsburgh. We were dressed in patch Swede jackets, with hip hugger pants also patchwork. Going to the club dressed alike was the thing to do back in 1971. Edward knew the bouncer at the door and he let us right in. We headed toward the VIP section where Edward's friends were waiting for us. At that time, I was drinking vodka and orange juice (I don't drink that anymore), and was well into my third drink when this chocolate chip, brown leather from head to toe walked through the door.

In my half-drunken haze, I said to Edward, "Man, he is fine."

He said, "Ila, you are not mine and never will be. Go for it."

My feet went cold. I had suspected he was gay, but didn't want to face the reality. That night, I left the Fantastic Plastic with the Chocolate Chip. Edward and I remained friends for many years after that night.

The door swung open and the nurse said, "Ila, please come with me."

We walked the green mile hallway to operating room two. I was told to take off all my clothes, leave them in a small changing area, and to meet the nurse on the other side of the door. I did as I was told. I met the nurse, walked over to the examination table, and was told I would be given a local anesthetic block. The lower part of my body would become numb in about ten minutes and the procedure would begin. What I remember so vividly is the pump. It sounded like a drum beat from an old thirty-three album. The procedure was over in approximately one hour. I was given some Darvon, a small box of Kotex and told to go home and rest. Another one of Ila's diamond was gone.

I took two Darvon and headed to Haines Point. I knew that I could find Hunter the weed man there if I waited long enough. I didn't want to go home without enough weed to keep me on a stupid high for the entire weekend. I drove from Virginia around the beltway to the park. I found a strategic place to park next to the Awakening statue. From that vantage point, I could see all traffic coming and going into the park, including the park police or the DC police. I knew that Hunter did most of his transactions there. I waited inside my car for about thirty minutes. This was the 70s; so wasting gas was not the thing to do with all of the gas lines. I turned the motor off and decided to sit on the park bench next to the Awakening Statue. Two hours later, I had given up, when a gray duce and a quarter drove slowly past me. I looked hard into the dark windows to see if it was Hunter. I spoke as the window rolled down. It was Rodney. I had not seen him since I drove him home therefore; I had no idea what kind of car he was driving.

He said, "You're the last person I expected to see here."

I said, "Same."

Are you waiting for someone?" he said.

I replied, "Yes, I'm waiting for a guy named Hunter. I'm sure you wouldn't know him."

He replied, "Hunter is on the other end of the park. I just left him."

I smiled and couldn't believe that the man who talked into his wrist also smoked weed.

He said, "Hunter and I have already hooked up. Do you think we could try our date again?"

I said, "actually, I just had an abortion and this isn't a good day. I just want to go home, get high, and play very slow tearing music."

He replied, "I have a better idea. Why don't you follow me to Southwest? I will draw you a bath, make you drinks until you pass out and cook you breakfast in the morning."

I said, "Thank you, but I don't have any personal items with me. I'd have to stop at the store."

He said, "I have every thing you need, including personal items and a tooth brush. Anything else you need?"

I said, "Nope," I got off the bench and followed him to Southwest.

He lived very close to where I started my life in DC on "G" street in a small enclave of townhomes. He had a designated parking space. I had to park on the street, which was hard to do in Southwest, but as grace would have it, I found a space near by. I could feel the blood coming out of my body and small cramping sensations began. I guess that Darvon was wearing off. I had five more. After that I would have to get the prescription filled.

His home was very comfortable and the decorating was done very tastefully. I am sure it cost a pretty penny to live in Southwest at that time, but he had to be near the White House, National Airport and the metro at all times while on duty. This was the perfect spot. I headed towards the couch because I was feeling really dizzy at that point. He led me to the bedroom, placed me on the bed, took off my shoes, pulled back the covers, gave me a huge blue towel, requested I strip, and then he told me he would make me a drink. I did as he requested, but by the time he came back, I was knocked out. It had been an exhausting day and I needed the comfort of someone else's home.

I woke up around 4:00 a.m. cramping and bleeding rather heavily. Rodney had stripped and gotten into the bed next to me. He was sleeping and didn't move as I exited the bed to clean myself up. I took another Darvon and got back into bed. I awoke again the next morning to the smell of pancakes, sausage, weed and orange juice. It was a crisp, fall,

Saturday morning and I was glad I had not gone home to wake up by myself. I went into the bathroom, and laid out was a washcloth, towel, toothbrush and hair comb. Oh, my, I was falling in love again. I laughed. After taking a quick shower, changing my Kotex, brushing my teeth, taking a Darvon, and combing my hair, I felt I was presentable enough to enter the kitchen. He was sitting on the small terrace eating pancakes, drinking coffee and juice and reading the paper. I walked out to the terrace and sat in the chair on the opposite side of the table. He smiled, told me I snored and that he left my pancakes in the oven. He said the syrup was on the counter and the juice was in the fridge. Coffee was on the counter also with cream and sugar. I started singing in my head, "What a man, what a man, what a mighty good man." Then I noticed the phone was off the hook. Too funny.

I was so hungry. I ate like a lumberjack. He had to make more pancakes. Any other woman would have been embarrassed, but not me. More pancakes, please. After sitting at the table for what seemed an hour, I got up, cleared the small table, put the dishes in the dishwasher and cleaned the rest of the kitchen. It was the least I could do for all of his hospitality. He had rolled a joint and left it in the ashtray on the terrace for me, while he took a shower. I sat on the terrace, smoked the joint and drank coffee. I was deep in thought about how I had gotten to this place in my life when he entered the terrace. He lit another joint and sat next to me without saying a word.

In what seemed like a very long time, he finally said, "Would you like to talk about it?"

I shook my head no. He got up, walked through the small living room into the kitchen, and placed the phone back on the hook. Within minutes, it rang. He answered and told the person on the other line that he had an assignment at 6:00 p.m. at the Air and Space Museum. He said that it would last approximately six hours.

I don't know what the other person said, but his reply was, "Okay, see you then."

I knew that was my exit phone call, so I slowly got up from the table to walk towards the bedroom.

He said, "Where are you going?"

I replied, "I've stayed too long at this party, and it's time to go home."

He said, "That phone call had nothing to do with you."

I said, "I know it had everything to do with me. If it were not for me, that person would be on their way over here."

I continued walking towards the bedroom and he followed. I sat on the bed, as he entered the bedroom. He removed his robe to put his lounging pants on, and what I saw made my heart stand still. There was no way I was going to leave that solid rock, solid. I knew I could not take him vaginally, but I was very creative with my tongue. A dick-sucking fiend friend named Diane had taught me. She was hooking in high school, but oh, that's another story. I got up from the bed, walked in front of him, and dropped to my knees. It didn't take him long to come. He was grateful and I thought that was payment in full. I got completely dressed, rolled another joint, kissed him goodbye, and thanked him for his hospitality. I got a wedding invitation from Rodney two weeks later!

It was New Year's Eve and I swore that I would not spend another New Year's Eve in the streets of Washington, DC, but there I was again at a stoplight on my way to another party. I had been praying for a special person to come into my life almost every night, but my prayers went unanswered. When we heard the gunshots and the horns blow, we got out of the car at the light, ran around the car and hugged each other. Yes, yet again, I was with my girlfriends on New Year's Eve.

After our moment of insanity, we continued to the party and found it in full swing in Hyattsville, Maryland. People were everywhere. The ladies didn't outnumber the men (thank goodness). It was going to be a great morning. The DJ, Bobby C., had everyone on the dance floor, with or without a partner. After visiting the bathroom at least two times, I was ready to party. Before I made my rounds at the party, every hair had to be in place, makeup just right and head tight. I made my way to the DJ table to request a dance song. DJ, Bobby C., asked me to write the song on a piece of paper along with my phone number. Ugh, he was fine, but I was not about to start another relationship. I was going to take my time (this time). I didn't want to go full out with anyone in this New Year. I was going to relax, concentrate on being promoted on my job, and give my libido a rest. I wrote down my request and gave him my work number. Then I walked away.

The party was slamming; I danced all night under the protective eye of DJ, Bobby C. Breakfast was about to be served. It was around 5:00 a.m. and the party was over at 6:00 a.m. I had taken my shoes off, and my hair had taken on a recess mode. But, everyone looked the same way and started to just chill, eat breakfast and drink champagne. Understand, we didn't even know whose party we were at. We got an invitation from a friend, who got it from a friend, so that was as good as getting it in the mail, right? Too funny. We enjoyed the evening like we were on the VIP guest list. As I looked around the room, I caught the eye of everyone but Teresa. The last time I saw her she was "doing the butt" and screamed when the song said, "Teresa got a big old butt." I went over to Shelley and Sabrina to see where Teresa could be. They, too, had not seen her since she was screaming about her "big old butt." I decided to take a look around the building to make sure she was all right. The building was pretty big, with two bar rooms, a pool table room, a backgammon and card game room, and some smaller alcoves. As I was rounded what I thought had to be the last alcove in the building, there was Teresa and DJ,

Bobby C. She had backed that big old butt up and he was riding. I slipped away and returned to the breakfast room. Twenty minutes later, here comes Teresa with her big old butt. I wished I could have retrieved that piece of paper I gave to Bobby C now, but it was too late. Teresa came to the table smiling from ear-to-ear. She looked like she had just been tossed and she ate like it. We laughed, clicked champagne glasses, and toasted to good health, wealth, and grace.

Once I dropped everyone off, it was about 9:00 a.m. All I wanted to do was shower, crawl into bed, and sleep the day away. As I entered my street, there were police cars everywhere. Drew was in handcuffs and Paula was on a gurney. I parked, ran to the ambulance, saw that Paula was bleeding, and was barely coherent. I asked the ambulance driver if I could accompany her for the ride to the hospital. Of course, I told him we were sisters.

He said, "Yes, hop in the front seat."

I did just that and actually enjoyed the spring air seat ride. I was praying for Paula and trying to remember phone numbers for Paula's mother and sister. As we entered the emergency room, I saw Paula's mother and sister. Someone had called them and they were a wreck not knowing how badly Paula was injured. They rushed her into the operating room and for what seemed like days, they worked on Paula to make her whole again. The doctor came into the waiting room to say that the stab wound was very deep, they had done all they could, and now all we could do was wait. Oh, my God! Wait, we did. I was working on no sleep, but hospital coffee is so strong, it gave me a real kick. Before I knew it, I was walking the halls of the hospital. I walked to the hospital gift shop, looked around, left there, went to the cafeteria, got more coffee, left there, and walked to the chapel. It had been sometime since I had actually gone to church, but my grandmother had taught me how to pray. I felt that now it was time to put my prayers to good use, and apply all that my grandmother had taught me. I stayed in the chapel for about thirty minutes, and then I returned to the waiting room. Paula had been placed into intensive care. I kissed her mother and sister goodbye and caught a cab back to my house. The only problem was that I didn't have enough money. As we turned the corner to my apartment, I saw the meter reading $25.00 and I had $15.00. Okay, now what? As he pulled up to the apartment building, I told him about what had happened and how I was short.

He said, "Here is my card. Send the money to the address on the back when you get it."

I got a small tear in my eye. It had been a long night and an even longer day. I thanked him, dragged myself up two flights of stairs, opened my door, and double locked it. I took all my clothes off while walking to the bedroom and managed to be completely naked as I walked through the bedroom door. I fell into the bed, and woke up the next morning when I heard the garbage trucks arriving. It was 7:00 a.m. I had to be at work at 8:30 a.m. I jumped up, showered, and placed my dress in the bathroom. I ran water so it would be steam pressed. Then I made instant coffee, ate an apple, placed the hot curlers on, and continued the ritual of getting dressed. My head was on fire, so I took two aspirin. Then I drank half a glass of juice, placed my tennis shoes on, put my pumps in a bag, and put my small purse from the weekend in my big purse. Then I remembered that I had no money. I had to go to my closet, and empty each purse until I accumulated four dollars. Ugh. I ran for the metro and finally relaxed.

Once at work, I entered my floor only to find it eerily silent. Especially after a holiday, usually everyone is in the hallway talking about his or her weekend. Then I saw the nurse. She was collecting urine. They did these surprise checks after long weekends to make sure that everyone didn't have that great a time. I turned around, headed back to the elevator, went to the lobby, and called my boss. I told him I was taking the Metro to the Pentagon to pick up a package for him that they called about last week.

He, of course, said, "Okay."

I walked out of the building to the Metro, hoping that the nurse would be gone by the time I got back, and she was.

I returned around 10:00 a.m. Things had settled down and people where off of pins and needles. It seems she only asked for two tests, and the persons she requested urine from were straighter than straight. My boss called me into his office around 10:30 a.m. He had been on the phone since I returned with the package. I entered his office with the package and his mail, date stamped. I had placed everything in order of necessity for him to read. I also gave him papers that required his signature, which had to have signature tabs and placed in folders in order of necessity. The red folder, he had to sign right away. The green folder was confidential material. The white folder was completely administrative, and the yellow folder could wait until tomorrow, if necessary.

I sat down for our weekly meeting of his calendar when he told me that we would be going on temporary duty (TDY) for three months and we had to leave on Friday. I was told only to pack comfortable clothes. We were going to a work campground and we would be working round the clock on a special project. I was only to tell my parents to call personnel if they needed to leave me a message. I was not prepared to go to TDY, but this job required me to travel at the drop of a hat. We covered his schedule, which included canceling everything already on the calendar for the next three months. I had to make sure that his private bills were paid before we left, and that birthday cards to the staff and special friends were sent out before we left. I had to make travel arrangements along with arranging for the receipt of vouchers for travel expenses. All this had to done in three days. I knew that this would be a late night and tomorrow would not be any better. I was glad we would not have to dress every day. If we had to dress everyday while on TDY, that meant I would have to get to the cleaners and pay for a two-day turn-around. Since he said it was casual, I could work that out.

There were no cell phones back in the day, so it was not about calling everyone from my cell phone to let them know I would be gone for three months. Of course, I took care of my boss's business first. After getting him squared away, I concentrated on what I would need. There were files to take, a tape recorder, and minimal supplies. I left the office that night at approximately 9:00 p.m. I thought I was the only one left in the building, but as I was leaving, I saw that there were many lights still on. The people at this place really loved their jobs, and for most, their jobs were their life. I walked slowly to the elevator, with my legs hurting from a day of ups and downs. I shuffled to the Metro, which wasn't good that time of night, but it was a beautiful winter evening. I was praying for the Lord to take care of me on this night.

I arrived home to find my message light on the phone blinking. I remembered that I had not checked my messages since New Year's Eve. I pulled off my clothes, put on a pot of hot water for tea, sat at the dining room table, and listened to my messages. Mom, sister, brother, and Rodney. Ugh. I returned the calls to my family to let them know that I would not be around for awhile. I made a list of things that had to be done—mail stopped, landlord prepaid and a trip to the bank would be necessary to cash travel checks. Previously, when I traveled, I would allow Paula to look after my car. She was still in intensive care but doing much better. I had spoken to her mother earlier in the day and told her I was going TDY and would not be back for a while. I wondered what was going to happen to their apartment. I didn't ask

I completed my list of things to do, made a cup of tea, pulled out my suitcase and began placing necessities into it.

I became very weary and wandered back to the bedroom when the phone rang.

"Hello," I said. "This better be good."

I answered that way because of the lateness of the hour. The voice on the other end hesitated.

"Hello, Ila? This is Phoenix's wife."

I could feel my body turn to granite.

"Yes," I said.

She replied, "I have a note here for you from Phoenix. I have been holding onto it for sometime. They found it with his personal affects."

I said, "Really?"

"Yes, really," she said with anger.

"Well," I said, "would you like to send it to me?"

"NO, I will not send it to you," she replied.

At that point, I thought to myself, the less said the better. I waited to hear whatever else she had to say.

After what seemed a lifetime, she said, "Inside the note was a check for $2,000.00. I just wanted you to know I am ripping it up."

I had no reply; I hung up the phone, and decided that as soon as I got back, I would get my phone number changed. Then I hoped that he didn't have the note addressed. No, he wouldn't have done that. But, she must have found his phone book. What is done in the dark, soon comes to the light. I got into bed and slept like someone had hit me on the head.

Thursday, I called my boss told him all the things I had to do, and he gave me a few more things to do. I got dressed, put my tennis shoes on. I walked to the bank, to the post office, and then to *Tire Kingdom*. I requested to speak to the manager. He came out, and I told him that I would be gone for three months. I asked if I could leave my car there, so it could be run and worked on at the same time. He wanted to charge me a holding fee.

I said, "I understand that you like to smoke a little bit."

He replied, "Yes, but only on special occasions."

I told him, "I have special occasion weed that needed a home while I'm gone."

He said, "The storage fee could be waived."

I walked away thinking, "Does everyone in Washington get high?" I smiled.

Walking back to my apartment, I thought I saw someone standing outside. I thought, well they are not waiting for me because everyone I know thinks I'm at work. As I got closer, I saw that it was Rodney. What in the world could he possibly want? Mr. Invitation. I walked slowly to the front door as he stood by his car.

He said, "Oh, you're not going to acknowledge me?"

I replied, "Is someone talking?"

He laughed and said, "I just came by to tell you that I will truly enjoy being on TDY with you."

I turned around and my jaw dropped to the ground. He laughed again.

Then he got in his car and said, "See you Friday morning."

Now that is just what I needed—Rodney on TDY for three months with me. I had not seen him since I received his wedding invitation in the mail. I sat for a minute and thought about how I was going to handle the TDY with Rodney around. Then it dawned on me. We would be so busy, Mr. Rodney wouldn't be an issue. I packed and repacked and went to bed. The limo was scheduled to arrive at 7:00 a.m. and then it would pick up my boss and drive us to the designated area where we would do our TDY for three months.

The next morning was beautiful and so full of promise. I took a quick shower, and smoked my last joint, because there would be no getting high on TDY. I curled my hair, drank a cup of coffee, dressed and soon the knock on the door came. It was the limo driver and Rodney (double Ugh).

He smiled his deep smile and asked me if he could help with my bags.

I smiled and replied, "No."

It was going to be a long ride to southern Virginia. Once in the limo, the driver provided coffee, with all the condiments, and pastries. Rodney helped himself. I got coffee and sat in silence.

Rodney finally said, "I didn't see you at the wedding. I looked for you to be there."

I replied, "Why in the world would I come to your wedding?"

He said, "Why in the world would you not?"

I felt his question didn't deserve a response. I sat in silence until we got to my boss's home. The limo driver walked to my boss's front door, and rang the bell. My boss was right there and ready in his dress uniform. I thought, that's funny, why does he have on his dress uniform? It was a quick thought in my mind at the time. Once we got to southern Virginia, it became clear why he had worn his dress uniform.

Once my boss was in the limo, it was all work. Plans were laid out for the three-month period and no notes were allowed to be taken. I tape-recorded our conversation so that I could remember everything he wanted Rodney and I to do. After everything was said and done, my boss laid back to relax. The ride would take about four hours, so we all settled in for mini naps.

Once at the facility, we checked in and were told to report to the main conference room for a briefing. Rodney and I had rooms next to each other. I am sure he pulled strings to make that happen. Be that as it may, we reported to the conference room for a briefing. All the huge brass was there, and now I knew why my boss had his dress uniform on. We were told this was a very secure assignment and we were not to leave the compound unless we had special permission, or unless it was a medical emergency. Other than that, everything anyone would need was on the compound. The work assignments were distributed and we were told to enjoy our evening because we had to report to work at 7:00 a.m.

I looked around the briefing room and was shocked to see that I was the only Black female on this assignment. I wondered why that seemed to be the case—not only here, but on most jobs—not that I felt it hindered me in any way. It would just be nice to hear another female say, "Hey, girl!" That would not be the case on this TDY and I had to get used to that.

It was almost dinnertime and everyone converged on the cafeteria, which was known to have great food. I ate salad only the first night. I had to be careful about my diet while I was on TDY. It was too easy to gain five to ten pounds due to all the starches and desserts. Of course, Rodney's plate looked like it belonged to three people. He sat down next to me in silence, grabbed my hand and placed it between his legs.

He said, "This is all yours for three months."

I got up and moved.

At the time, we didn't have Internet; it was interoffice net only. We had special permission to have the interoffice net connected to our TDY computers so that communication would be live and well between the TDY team and the main office. This would help a great deal. I could keep up with daily correspondence and calendar inputs for my boss. Just because we were on TDY, the rest of the world didn't stop.

I went to the small office they had designated for me at approximately 8:00 p.m. I wanted to put the office in working order before tomorrow. I connected to the interoffice net, checked messages, returned messages on the phone mail, and prepared my workspace to begin work in the morning. I felt someone standing in the doorway and I knew it was Rodney. Shouldn't he be guarding someone?

"Rodney, what do you want?" I said.

He replied, "It's happy hour, and you know they have the best top shelf for all the big wigs. You're going to show your face, right?"

I thought about that for a minute and said, "Yes, I guess I should. Give me a couple of minutes and I will meet you there."

He sat down…

"Rodney, please," I said. "I'll meet you there."

"I want to talk to you," he said. "We left a lot of loose ends."

I listened. He sounded like a Prince song—"I only want to see you laughing in the Purple Rain." Too funny. I sat and listened to his tale about how he got his girlfriend pregnant, and she happened to be the Jamaican ambassador's daughter. He told a story of how she enchanted him and how her father set them up after he was on detail to guard him at a special assignment. After the special assignment, he called and requested his presence at a formal dinner party at his home in Chevy Chase, Maryland. Of course, being a secret service person, you didn't turn down those invitations. He attended, was introduced to the ambassador's daughter and the rest is history. He had a wife and a son on the way really soon.

The happy hour was in full swing when we arrived at around 9:00 p.m. I went to the bar only to find my boss about five shades to the wind. I asked him if he needed help to his room.

He said, "Yes."

I got Rodney and we escorted my boss to his room, which ended up being a nightly ritual, while we were on TDY. I had not realized he had a drinking problem. I knew he liked scotch a lot, but not that much. I felt there was more going on than he was letting us know about. Like any good military person, I only took orders and kept my head low. My boss would tell me later if there was anything, I should know. Rodney removed his dress uniform and placed him in the shower. I left and went to my room.

I was exhausted. I took a shower, washed my hair, made tea on the hot plate, and called it a night. I thought. About 2:00 a.m. there was a knock on the door. It was Rodney.

I told him, "Go back to your room. It's late and we have to get up early."

He said through the door, "I don't want to be alone."

I opened the door. He was drunk. He took off his clothes, and got into the extra full bed. He was snoring before I could turn off the lights. It was going to be a long three months.

At 6:00 a.m., I got Rodney out of my room and sent him to his room. I showered and went down to the cafeteria for breakfast. Everyone looked a little green around the edges. I looked for my boss and didn't see him. I left the cafeteria, walked to his room and began banging on the door. It took a few minutes but he answered.

"Are you all right?" I asked.

He replied, "Ugh," using my terminology.

I laughed and told him, "Hurry up so you can at least have breakfast."

I walked back to the cafeteria and ran into Rodney. He looked as if nothing had happened last night. He had his secret service look on and nothing else mattered. We walked in silence to the cafeteria, ate breakfast in silence, and we went our separate ways to start our day of work.

As I opened up my interoffice net, there was an emergency bulletin that had to be opened right away. The bulletin announced that Admiral Baxter had shot himself in his office overnight and that a day office custodian had found the body. Oh, my God, what a way to start the day. I ran to the cafeteria hoping my boss would be there by now, but it was clear that everyone had gotten the notice, including my boss. He motioned me over and told be to find Rodney. He said they would be leaving the compound in one hour. He told me I had to stay. I was very close to Admiral Baxter and I knew that this TDY would keep me from being at his funeral or seeing his family during their time of bereavement. I found Rodney in his office, and I told him what had happened. He immediately reported to the cafeteria for further instructions from my boss. A member of our team had to be left behind, I was the logical choice.

The days and nights were endless with file reading, shredding and dismantling of files. I had so many paper cuts that my hands looked like a war zone. The only saving grace about this TDY was happy hour and I had time to catch up on my reading—I mean reading for fun, not for work. I had bought the latest Patricia Cornwell novel about two months before and had not had time to read it. I also had the *Fire Next Time* by James Baldwin that I was determined to finish, and a periodical on tattoos—something that I always wanted to get but never had the nerve. I wanted to do some research on the entire trade before I made up my mind where and when I was going to have it done.

Almost two weeks later, Rodney and my boss returned. I missed everything. Admiral Baxter was buried at the national cemetery and it was on television. There were many cocktail receptions and people came from all over the world to show their respects. Rodney said he worked day and night, but met some very nice people and said he got a chance to see his wife.

I had started an exercise routine every morning at 5:30 a.m. It was approximately three miles around the compound, so every morning I forced myself to get up and walk the compound before the day began. This would be the beginning of a lifelong routine of walking every day. It's funny how lifetime habits start. Of course, as soon as Rodney found out I was walking, he had to come with me, with his half-naked self. He ran more than he walked, so he was not a big distraction. I know he just wanted to have someone to talk to. To be honest, I was glad he was back.

Rodney and I spent every night together. It turned out he was addicted to porn, so he had brought his entire collection with him on VHS. The TV provided in each room only took VHS tapes to be used for training. So every night we drank, masturbated, and went to bed.

We finished our TDY on a Friday. I was ready to get back to my apartment, use my own bathroom, and relax in my own bed. I put Rodney out of my room. I put on a robe and walked to my boss's room to make sure he was up. Then I went back to my room to finish packing. I was at the gate waiting when they arrived. We rode home in silence. I was dropped off first because I lived in Virginia. My boss gave me the weekend off and laughed.

"See you Monday," he said.

Rodney just nodded. The next day, I received a dozen red roses from Rodney with a card that said, "The best roommate ever, Love Rodney." Extremely funny.

When I woke up, it was Saturday evening. I felt like I had been in a coma. I was starving and I knew there was absolutely nothing in the refrigerator to eat because I had been gone so long. I opened the refrigerator and sure enough, margarine, bad orange juice, old eggs, and things with lots of fuzz. I cleaned it all out except the margarine, because that stuff lasts forever. I then opened the freezer to find vegetable lasagna, and a smile came over my face. I heated the stove and popped the lasagna in. It would take approximately forty minutes to heat up and another ten minutes to cook all the way through. I figured since I could smell myself, I should take a shower, wash my hair, and shave my legs and underarms. I did do those things while I was away, but it seems you always miss spots when you are not in your own bathroom with your own lighting. After staying in the shower for at least forty minutes, I could smell the lasagna from the kitchen, and my mouth watered. I was hungry. As I walked to the kitchen, I could still see the red light jumping on my answering machine. I think I saw fifty messages on the light as I walked through on Friday night. I had to eat first. I could listen to the messages later. It was time for the quiet storm on WHUR and that gorgeous host with those beautiful gray eyes, Donnie Simpson. That radio show was either just what I needed for a calm and uneventful evening, or else I could commit suicide—depending upon where my mind was on any given night. Once he started playing, "Blue Magic's Side Show," or "Once In My Lifetime," by Phyllis Hyman, it either brought back good memories or bad ones. It seemed that there was no in between. Tonight, I was in a very nostalgic mood and the songs felt good for my soul.

After eating what I thought surely was a gourmet meal, I separated my clothes for the Sunday morning wash in the basement. I vowed that if I ever bought my own home, the first thing I would buy would be my own washer and dryer. As it was, either I would have to get up at the crack of dawn to do laundry, or I'd have to wait until midnight so I wasn't disturbed. I decided that early morning would be better since I was still very tired. I again walked past the blinking light on the answering machine, vowing to return calls the next day.

I didn't have a TV in my bedroom because I have always felt that the bedroom was for lovemaking, reading, and conversation. There was no place in the bedroom for a TV. It was easy to fall asleep in my bedroom. It had candles, and was painted in hues of brown, beige and mauve. It also had books, incense, and of course, weed, when I had it. Tonight, I didn't need books, candles, or weed. I was knocked out once again until early morning. Since the time had changed, it was getting light very early. I awoke to the sun at about 6:30 a.m., got right up and beat the Sunday morning paper and coffee crowd in the basement. By 11:00 a.m., it would be crowded and it would be early afternoon before I finished my laundry. I had, thank God, separated all my things the night before and placed them in three separate baskets. I got the washing powder, a cup of coffee that I had to drink black, and I quickly put on a pair of old slacks, a sweatshirt, and slippers. I found my keys and I was out the door. As I turned to lock the door, I heard a very loud noise below. I looked down the staircase and there they were—Paula and Drew, hand in hand and wasted. That was so funny. When I left, Paula had been in intensive care and Drew was on his way to jail. I screamed their names and they looked up.

Then they started screaming, "Where have you been? Let's get high."

I explained to them that I had a lot of laundry to do and getting high was not in the picture right now.

Drew pulled out a fat joint from his coat pocket and said, "Toke on this when you get a minute, and come over when you're done."

Paula said, "Boy, we missed you."

I laughed, told them both to get some sleep, and that I would see them later.

It took several hours to finish my clothes. I ran out of quarters and had to walk to the store and get change. While I was there, I got some provisions and a Sunday paper. My intentions were good, but I still didn't finish the laundry until 1:00 p.m. By that time I had gone to the store, remembered I had to pick up my car from *Tire Kingdom* before noon, the laundry room was full and everyone wanted to know where I had been. So, lying and laughing, it was 2:30 p.m. before I got back upstairs to my apartment.

I entered the living room with my last basket of clothes and there it was—the blinking light. Okay, it was time to listen to my messages. I had picked up a bottle of German Riesling while at the store and had placed it in the freezer. It was ready. I uncorked it, and pulled a tall glass, got the joint, sat at the table and listened to my messages. I called my family and my girls to let them know I was back. I wrote down the other messages. I would return those phone calls during the week. The joint was very powerful. I couldn't smoke it all and the wine was slowly going to my head. I put the radio on and began to fold my clothes. Then I put them away. I heard a knock on the door. Okay, I thought, it must be Paula or Drew, but by the way they looked, I thought they would be knocked out for the rest of the afternoon. I looked through the peephole and it was Rodney. I waited.

He shouted, "I know you are in there. I brought a peace offering."

I slowly opened the door and there he was, looking all chocolate and fine. He was holding a bag of carryout from my favorite Chinese restaurant. He also had a bottle of German Riesling. OK, I could not resist. I let him in and I was very hungry. It had been a long time since I ate the vegetable lasagna. We spread out everything on my small dining room table, General Tso, Hunan Chicken, spring rolls, noodles and hot tea. Perfect. We ate and talked, ate and talked, and ate and talked. There was so much we could not talk about while we were on the compound. We laughed at the people and some of the assignments we were given. We ate almost everything. There was not much to clean up. He looked at me and then looked at the television in the living room. I told him to help himself. I told him I was going to finish putting my laundry away and clean my room. There was a lot of dust in there after being gone for three months. I was in my room about thirty minutes when I re-entered the living room and found Rodney fast asleep. I covered him and went back to my bedroom, lit a candle, finished my joint, and cleaned the rest of my room.

Rodney woke up around 8:00 p.m. and went into the bathroom. Before I knew it, I heard the water running in the shower. No, he didn't! But, you know he was that kind of guy that I couldn't stay mad at. I overlooked the shower and went back to my reading. Rodney came out of the shower dripping wet with a look of lust in his eyes. I wasn't ready to have a relationship with Rodney. If I did, it would be very complicated. He was married only a short time and I really didn't want to get tied up with yet another married man. He came into the bedroom. He dried off, put his boxer shorts back on, and got into bed, and feel asleep. Too funny. I guess he feels the same way I do. I let him sleep until 11:00 p.m. He woke up, got dressed, and thanked me for my hospitality. Then he left. The phone rang as he was walking out the door.

He said, "Never accept a call from a man after 11:00 p.m., because it's just a bootie call."

That was the first time I had heard that expression. I laughed and he left. I didn't answer the phone.

That Monday morning, it was cold. The metropolitan area could really get cold and wet during the fall and winter months. I had to pack up my office today and report to my new position. I was very excited. My new position required more travel, but it would be in the field of training. I was excited about the opportunity to learn new things and meet new people.

The move went pretty smoothly. Rodney helped me move a lot of boxes and the building maintenance people took care of the other heavier items. I was on good terms with all the support staff, so getting my office moved was no problem. After they finished, I ordered eight pizzas, soda, and gave them each ten dollars. Those guys worked hard and had to move offices, furniture, home furnishings, etc., at the drop of a hat. Anytime a ranking official moved, they had to be there to make sure it happened. They were a great group of guys, and I wanted them to know how much I appreciated their work and seeing them everyday. It was really nice to see the brothers on the maintenance team, the sisters in the cafeteria, and on the cleaning staff. I made sure that they all got Christmas bonuses, words of encouragement, and a thank you. That was important to me.

My office was in a huge suite. The four star general had an exclusive office with a private bathroom that had a tub and a shower. His office overlooked a park and the windows were tinted. His computer and electronic devices had to be placed on an inside wall. They were very cognizant about information being able to be picked up through the air. My office was located off to the right through a door. It didn't take me long to understand that the door was not to be closed unless he had a meeting. He didn't like to use the intercom; so calling my name was what he did all day. My other boss was very computer and gadget friendly, but this man, didn't think for himself.

Our first week was a bit difficult. He wanted breakfast and lunch brought to his office. He didn't go out for either unless they were for meetings. He wanted me at work at 8:30 a.m., and he expected me to be there until 6:00 p.m. or longer, if necessary. All his travel arrangements were to be made and booked first class. He didn't take taxis. A driver had to be available to him at all times. Dates of all his families' birthdays and friends had to be recorded and I had to buy and wrap presents in a timely fashion. He gave me a credit card to *Dillards* and *Hechts*. He made arrangements to have me notated as a second signer on the cards and those cards were to be used for all his personal purchases. The bills came to the office and I was responsible for making sure that he paid them on time.

The computer system had been improved with this move. His calendar came up on my computer every morning. At the end of each day, I was to give him an itinerary for the next day. If there were meetings he couldn't attend the next day, I had to stay until the meetings had been cancelled and rearranged. His shirts were to be picked up from the laundry every week and paid for through petty cash. He would reimburse the petty cash box at the end of each month. All his personal items in the bathroom should never run out. It was my responsibility to make sure that the bathroom, mini bar, and refrigerator was stocked at all times. At no time should his office be depleted of candy and coffee. I had to brew coffee twice a day if he was in town. Okay, those were the ground rules. Now for the other stuff.

I had to make sure everyone on the training staff was prepared and ready to go, which included making travel arrangements. I had to verify and keep track of the courses they were taking. I also had to track the requirements for their positions and notate their progress. If they were taking courses outside of the ones offered at the company, I had to track those courses since they couldn't be reimbursed unless they received a C or better in the course. Also, the young men who were in surveillance training had to be housed for the time they were in training, and relocated after the training was over. Okay, I had received a $5,000.00 increase, but this was $10,000.00 worth of additional work. I was up for the challenge. I didn't have any reason not to succeed in this new position. The ground rules were very clear.

Time was passing by so fast. This new position didn't leave a lot of time for dating or going out. I worked at least two weekends every month. That meant that long weekend trips were out of the question. Rodney somehow got assigned to the four star general. I don't know how he managed to get that position, but there he was on my third week at the job. As he strutted towards me, he looked like a black diamond. He had gotten really buff, had lost about fifteen pounds, and he looked so good. He and his wife had had a baby boy who they named Rodney Taylor II. He showed me pictures of their beautiful baby boy. His wife wanted more children, but Rodney was very satisfied with one child. Rodney's office was just down the corridor so he spent a lot of time at or around my desk. The general was escorted everywhere, so Rodney had to be available at the drop of a hat. He got the general's schedule everyday and accompanied him to meetings, lunch appointments, dinner appointments and various rendezvous appointments. Confidentiality was so important in his job. That is why he kept getting promoted. He was good at his job and could look like one of the crowd so easily. He was a great marksman and received numerous awards from the secret service. I was proud of him. He was one of the few Black men in the secret service at the time, and he carried himself with dignity and respect. I was the only one there who knew he was addicted to porn and loved to masturbate. Extremely funny.

Rodney came to me on a Monday afternoon, and said, "Are you ready?"

I said, "What are you talking about?"

He replied, "You're going on surveillance training because you're the only black female in the training section."

I said, "all the men already know who I am. We couldn't pull off surveillance with them, without me being picked up on the street."

He said, "I don't know. That's the word on the street. I guess we'll see after our staff meeting today."

I said, "You're crazy and you just want me to be running around Washington, DC like a homeless person."

He laughed and walked away.

Our staff meetings were always set for 4:00 p.m. on Mondays. If the general was out of town, he would do it by conference call, but it was never to be cancelled. If I was on leave, I had to get someone to cover the conference call. That was one good thing about having Rodney around. He would take care of those things if I needed to take a day off. We began the conference call on this day at exactly 4:00 p.m. The staff meeting consisted of one, four star general, two, two star generals, three deputies, Rodney, and myself. At the end of the meeting, I was told to get ready to go on TDY for three months for surveillance training. The lady who had my job previously was instructed to man the office until I returned. I tried very hard not to show my disappointment. I had only been in the position four months and really liked the job because it was different every day. I waited until everyone left and requested an audience with my boss.

He said right away, "I know, you don't want to go. But this will be an experience you will never forget. If you turn it down, it will never be offered to you again. So you go home and sleep on it. Let me know your answer in the morning. Remember, you will be staying in the best hotels in the metro area, driving the best cars, and gaining working knowledge that you could never pay for."

I thanked him and left his office. I returned to my desk and the phone was ringing. It was Rodney.

He said, "Well, I guess you should at least go to bed with me before you leave."

I hung up on him. I could hear his laughter from down the hall, as he got an earful of the dial tone.

There was a restaurant not far from the company where I could go for happy hour. I felt today was a good day to stop by, have a drink, and think about this great opportunity I had been given. I walked to the *Top of the Tower*, and happy hour was in full swing. It was two for one; so getting your head right didn't take long. They had a buffet of Swedish meatballs, baby quiche, chicken drummets, a vegetable and fruit platter, and bottled water. The buffet was never empty and happy hour went from 5:00 p.m. until 7:00 p.m. I walked to the first empty seat I could find. I was glad it was near a window so I could gaze out and think while drowning my sorrows. As I sat and thought about the pros and cons of going on this TDY, a young man approached me. I had seen him sitting at the bar as I walked past, but I thought he was waiting for someone.

He said, "Excuse me, are you waiting for someone?"

I replied, "No."

He said, "May I take a seat?"

I said, "I'm not sure this is the day to try to make friends with me."

He replied, "I'll take my chances." Then he asked, "What are you drinking?"

I replied, "Hennessy straight, with a water back."

He said, "WOW, a strong drink for such a young lady."

My reply was, "Be careful who you call a lady."

He laughed. We sat in silence for what seemed like forever. He finally told me that his name was LeRoy Wright. He was a bank manager for *First Union Bank.* He had just moved here from Atlanta and was finding Washington difficult. I told him about all the hot spots that he could go to and the names of the guys at the doors. I told him that usually if you could address the doorman by name, getting in the door was no problem. He was surprised to hear I knew all the spots.

He said, "Your looks are deceiving. You look very conservative and surely not the type to go clubbing."

I told him, "Looks are very deceiving, and you should never judge a woman by her *Nine West* pumps."

He laughed, and that cut the ice. Before I knew it, they were taking away the buffet, and happy hour was over. LeRoy was very attractive, but he was a very light-skinned brother with gray eyes. He just wasn't my type. I liked men toasted brown. He was very interesting, had been born and raised in Chicago, went to Morehouse, graduated with a degree in business, tried working for himself for several years, and finally ended up in the banking business. He had done very well in the new financial planning area of the bank. At that time, they were just getting into offering IRA's and Certificates of Deposits. He had taken an American Express Financial crash course and took that knowledge to the bank.

He also said that he was a great dancer and that he'd love to go out with me sometime.

As the waitress cleared our table, I told him that we should leave before they put us out. They were getting ready for the late dinner crowd and wanted all the Happy Hour patrons to either stay and eat or go home. We walked to the elevator together, talking non-stop. I was very interested at this point even though I didn't find him attractive. I thought he would make a great friend. We exchanged cards on the street. I took a seat on a statue and changed my shoes, to make the walk to the metro. I was taking the orange line and he was going to get his car. He offered me a ride home, but I decided not to let him know where I lived until we got to know each other better. I refused his offer and told him that I hoped he would call later in the week. At that point, he kissed me on the cheek and walked away.

As I walked in the door, my phone was ringing. It was my friend Sheila. She wanted to go to the Carter Baron over the weekend to see Frankie Beverly and Maze. The tickets were going fast. She asked if I wanted in. I said I would love to go, but I was broke. I told her I would call her right back. I called LeRoy and told him that we were thinking about going to the Carter Baron to see Frankie Beverly and Maze and did he want to go, and buy my ticket.

He laughed and said, "Well, how can I say no? Okay, it's a date. I'll meet you at the will call office at 6:00 p.m. because the show starts at 7:00 p.m."

I called Sheila back, told her I had a sponsor and that I would pick her up at 5:00 p.m. on Saturday.

She laughed, and said, "Cool."

I knew it wouldn't be long before I would have to "cock or walk" with LeRoy. But, I was going to string it out as long as possible. It was not until we were together that Saturday night that he decided to tell me he was married. Not only married, but also married with two children. His wife worked for United Airlines as a flight attendant. I knew this was a number I could drop in the toilet when I got home. I was not about to get mixed up with yet another married man. I wanted to be married myself one day, and couldn't imagine having to wonder where my husband was on a Saturday night. I go along to get along, so I didn't make a scene. It was a relationship for the night and I would send payment for the ticket in the mail to his job. He would surely get the idea that I was not interested after that. I decided to worry about it later and have a good time. As I started to stand up and sing all the words to "Happy Feeling," a joint came down the row. I usually passed on passed joints, because you never knew what you would get. I passed it to Sheila.

She took a hit and said, "Girl, just one puff."

I said," Okay."

For sure, one puff was great, but two puffs, well, that made everything all right. I passed it to LeRoy who passed it on, but I noticed he had been drinking ginger ale very slowly since we had arrived. I later discovered that he was drinking Jack Daniel's and ginger ale. Everyone had a reason to be numb in Washington, DC. You just had to pick your poison. LeRoy excused himself during intermission. I was still in the afterglow of that joint and listening to Frankie sing everything I wanted to hear. The second half would be icing on the cake. The show started, we looked around for LeRoy, but he was gone. I began to worry that maybe he had gotten drunk and needed help. Sheila convinced me that he had probably run into people he knew and couldn't come back to our seats. LeRoy never returned. The concert was excellent. Sheila and I waited for the crowd to thin out before we headed to my car. As we were exiting the entrance gate, we saw him standing at the gate, drunk; I mean really drunk. Ugh, that is all I needed—a married drunk. I walked over to him and asked if he could drive home.

He said, "No."

I looked at Sheila. She got on one side of him and I got on the other. We walked him to my car. He got into the back seat and lost his cookies all over my leather seats. Damn. I got out and opened the trunk to get some rags. Then I pulled him out of the back seat. I cleaned it up the best I could. Then I placed him back into the back seat. Somehow we got his address in Hyattsville, Maryland. It was out of my way. Sheila said she had nothing to do and the ride would do her good. Fortunately, one of my club sisters lived in Hyattsville, so I was very familiar with the area.

He slurred, "Turn here, left here."

Soon, we were on his street—Raydale Road. I asked him if he wanted us to walk him to the house.

He said, "No."

Sheila told him that we would just tell his wife that his car would not start and we offered him a ride.

"Okay," he said.

We drove him to the door. He got out, stumbled up the steps and placed the key in the door. I drove off like a Daytona Speedway racer. I didn't want his wife to get a glimpse of my car.

We laughed at LeRoy all the way to Virginia.

Sheila said, "Drive into Haines Point and see if Hunter is around. I'm completely out of weed."

I did and there he was by the statue, a real businessman. The park was officially closed, but driving through was not prohibited; stopping was prohibited. I never saw Hunter's car, and never knew how he got in or out of the park. I guess that was the point. He gave Sheila a lid, and looked at me. I told him I was broke. He handed me a half-lid and told us to move on. He said that he would see us both on payday. As we drove off, he made a notation in his little brown book.

We crossed the 14th Street Bridge, and I dropped Sheila off on Arlington Boulevard, then I hurried home.

Sunday was a clear day and it was warming up as the seasons had turned from winter to early spring. There was nothing like the metropolitan area in early spring. The cherry blossoms were blooming and flowers were peeping through the grass. A new group of college graduates and trainees would be coming to the company on Monday to be trained for two weeks. This would be my last class until I went on TDY. I wouldn't be able to meet the next class. I was still a little apprehensive about the surveillance position for three months. However, as my boss said, if I ignored this temporary duty (TDY) there wouldn't be another opportunity. I had pretty much resigned myself to going and making the best of it. It would be an opportunity to learn another area in the company. This morning I missed my confidant Phoenix. He would advise me on this TDY situation and he was always right. He had been in the community for sometime and knew the right steps to take to get ahead. I missed him at the midnight hour.

As Sunday morning turned into Sunday afternoon, I took a shower. I pulled on some old jeans, a sweatshirt, old tennis shoes and prepared myself to walk to the drug store for a newspaper and a cup of coffee from the *7-Eleven*. It would taste much better than the instant coffee I had in the cabinet. I went to grab my jacket when there was a knock at the door. I couldn't believe the people who felt that they didn't have to call before they came to my home. I looked through the peephole, and saw Rodney. I opened the door and there he stood with the paper, a large cup of coffee with vanilla flavored cream, and bagels. I could fall in love with this guy. He came in, placed everything on the dinette table, took off his coat, and laid it on the couch. He turned on the television and began watching college basketball—the one sport I really loved. I fell right in, pulled my tennis shoes off, got on the floor with my huge pillow and enjoyed the bagels, coffee and the company. Before I knew it, I was asleep. When

I woke up, the game was over. Rodney had put in one of his VHS tapes and was going at it. I laughed and asked if he was staying for dinner.

With a grimace, he said, "Yes."

Rodney left after dinner and said he would see me in the morning. I washed my hair, turned on the *Quiet Storm*, read a book, and went to bed.

I got up at 6:00 a.m., took a walk around the block to start my day, came back, took a shower, dressed and had to run to the metro. This was going to be a busy day and that 8:30 a.m. start time was giving me a real headache. Once at my desk, things were really busy. Students and agents checking in, classes and workshops starting, and people running through the corridors who didn't want to miss the start of a new workshop or class. Around 11:00 a.m. it slowed down. Everyone was in his/her class or workshop, had been signed in, clearances received, and badges given out. It was a lot of work, but also so much fun. We had people there from all over the world. I thanked my creator everyday for the opportunities he had given me. A girl from Homewood in Pittsburgh, Pennsylvania was all the way in Washington and interacting with people from all over. It was a dream job come true.

After things settled, I went into the general's office to see what he wanted for lunch. I was surprised that I had not heard from him most of the morning. He knew my undivided attention had to be on registration. One wrong person in the wrong class and with the wrong clearance could compromise a great deal. He was sitting on the couch looking very sick. I ran and got the garbage can, and it seemed in minutes he was losing his cookies into the basket. Boy, did it stink. I called Rodney on the intercom; he rushed to the office, got a mop and bucket from the maintenance office, and cleaned up the mess. The general missed the basket a couple of times. Rodney got the general a clean shirt, washed his face, and made him walk to the back elevator. The elevator went straight to the parking lot, and the elevator could only be accessed by using a card key. Rodney placed his card key into the slot, the elevator opened, and they disappeared. I finished cleaning the office. Then I called the administrator and told him that the general had the flu and Rodney was taking him home.

He said, "Security's been notified, but keep me informed of the general's status."

The afternoon went by without incident. Rodney returned to say he had placed the general in bed and his wife was taking good care of him.

It was unfortunate that the general had gotten sick, but my life was much easier when he was not there bellowing out my name every hour. I did keep in touch with him by phone approximately every four hours, because that's what he wanted. He also had the interoffice e-mail system at home, so e-mails were coming fast and furious. As anal as he was, he was a great boss. He never forgot to bring me chocolate from Brussels, Nike tennis shoes from Korea, and purses from France and Italy. In addition, he always brought perfume from Switzerland. On holidays, he would have me purchase a piece of jewelry for myself using the credit cards he provided. For my birthday, he always purchased a round trip ticket for me to go to Pittsburgh.

He always said, "You should go home once a year to appreciate where you are now."

The two weeks of training classes went extremely fast. The young men from MIT, Harvard, Yale, Northwestern, and Ohio State were very nice and eager to work for the company. I was excited to know that I would see them in a shopping mall or in a grocery store and could not even acknowledge their presence. Doing so would jeopardize them and their families. I collected stamps from all over the world and they would send stamps to me via airplane courier. The collection is probably worth a great deal of money by now.

Once the last student left, I microfiched their identities, and shredded all paper records. I began to think about the TDY that was scheduled to begin that next week. I began getting my desk in order. The lady who was taking my place would love to find out something on me or show the general that I had done something wrong. It took the entire week to balance petty cash, and to make sure the general's personal affairs were taken care of in advance. The cleaners would have someone pick up the cleaning in the lobby. The general just had to leave it there in the morning and someone would bring it back in the evening. The cafeteria staff said they would take care of breakfast and lunch while I was gone. The supervisor said she would send someone up to take his order each day. WOW, that is why it pays to be nice to people. The lady who would fill in for me had just been taken out of the day-to-day picture. I locked my calendar with a password, so she only had access to the general's calendar. I had to have the combinations to my safes changed and my security badges changed. I now worked for the State Department according to my credentials. At the end of the week, I turned my keys over to the young lady, said goodbye to the general and other staff members. Then I left the building.

On Monday morning, I would be headed for yet another adventure. On Saturday morning, I had to start my day very early. I went to the post office to have them stop my mail. I paid my landlord three months in advance. I took all of my cleaning to the cleaners, and paid in advance to have them ready for pick-up by 8:00 p.m. that evening. I was about to throw away everything in my refrigerator when it dawned on me that Paula and Drew were always looking for something to eat. I called Paula. She came right over and took everything.

She would always ask me, "Where you going?" and I would always tell her, "I'm going out of town for a few weeks. See you when I get back."

She handed me two large joints and said, "Keep your head bad," and laughed.

I was grateful for the joints I needed bargaining power at the Tire Kingdom. I drove over negotiated with the manager, gave him the joints and walked home. Once again, all I had in my refrigerator was breakfast food and orange juice, cold Absolut, bottled water, and an open bottle of German Riesling.

I began packing my clothes for the very long TDY stay. I was not sure exactly what to carry. This would be the first TDY where I did surveillance on the students that I should have been registering for classes. I knew there would be a great deal of outside work required, so coats, sweaters, jeans, and boot shoes, seemed to be the things to pack. If I needed formal wear or other clothes, it would have to come out of my per diem, which was very generous. I had to go to the security office on Monday morning to pick up my assignment and the address of where I'd be living for the next three months. In the meantime, I made an afternoon breakfast, got high, and packed.

It was around 6:00 p.m. when the phone began to ring so insistently. Whoever it was hung up and called right back since I wasn't answering the phone. I thought it was that crazy Rodney and I was determined not to play house with him today. On the third call, I answered it.

"Hello?"

"Hello," said the voice on the other end. "This is LeRoy."

I was shocked. I had not given him any home information—just work information. Oh, but I banked at First Union. No, he didn't...I was silent.

Then he said, "I know it is against all regulations, but I took a shot to see if you were a First Union customer. There you were—phone number and address."

I was still silent.

He said, "I was wondering if you would like some company on this Saturday evening, or if you would like to go out for a drink."

I replied, "I'm packing to go on a vacation."

He offered to help me pack.

I said, "No."

He offered to get dinner and bring it over.

I said, "No."

He said, "Boney James is playing at the WC Bone Restaurant. I've got tickets to the 10:00 p.m. show. Would you like to go?"

Oh, he is a slick one. I guess in his drunken haze, he remembered that I liked jazz.

At that point I said, "Yes, what time should I be ready?"

He said, "I'm on the corner in a public phone. I'll wait at your apartment until you're ready."

I hesitated. Boney James.

"Okay," I replied. "Come on over."

Of course, it was only a few moments before he was at the door. I answered the door and let him in. He looked around with a frown. My apartment was a mess because I was packing and getting ready for my trip. I told him that I had been packing and re-packing, and apologized for the look of the apartment.

I took his coat and hung it up. Oh my! He did look good—brown wool slacks, slight cuff, with an off-white shirt, starched and brown stone cufflinks. His jacket was brown herringbone. Damn. I had no idea what I was going to wear. All my clothes were at the cleaners and were supposed to be picked up by 8:00 p.m. Fortunately, they were open for a half-day on Sunday. But I had paid in advance so I was not really concerned. I didn't want to offer him a drink, so I offered him breakfast because that was all I had in my refrigerator. He thanked me but declined. He did ask if I had anything to drink. I told him I had a cold bottle of Absolut. He requested that I place it on the rocks. At that point, I decided to keep my drinking to a minimum. I might have to be the designated driver before this night was over. Time was ticking by, so I placed all my clothes in the middle of the floor, and put on the radio and television; I told him that I would be ready in thirty minutes. He nodded his head and turned towards the television.

I quickly took a shower and curled my hair with the hair dryer. I glanced into my closet, pulled out a chocolate brown knit dress, brown boots and a black wrap. I placed these items on the bed and went back into the bathroom to complete my makeup and my hair. I heard the refrigerator open up so I knew he was on his second drink. Yes, there was no question in my mind that I would be driving this evening. Forty-five minutes later, I was ready and he was feeling no pain. I told him that I would be driving and he didn't object. He gave me his keys. What I didn't know was that he drove an Audi 5 speed. It had been a long time since I had driven a stick shift vehicle. This should be a date to remember. The Audi was plush and the sound system was fantastic. It didn't take long to get the hang of the five-speed; before I knew it we were taking Route 50 into DC and cruising at a safe speed. He requested that I stop at an ABC store. I knew there was one on the corner of Route 50 and Arlington Boulevard, so I took that exit. He appeared to be smiling deeper as we drove into the parking lot of the ABC store. As he got out of the car, I wondered what I had gotten myself into. It was going to be a long night. He came out of the ABC store with a cold bottle of Absolut and a cup that said, "Know your ABC's." Clever. He immediately broke the seal and began his long decent into a drunken stupor.

By the time we got to WC Bone, I knew he would not be awake for the entire show. As we walked to the front door, a line had formed and who was standing in line but Rodney and his wife. I turned to look the other way, but he felt it was the perfect opportunity to meet my date and to introduce me to his wife. He walked towards me holding his wife's hand.

"Hi," he said. "Honey, this is Ila and Ila this is my wife, Jackie."

I said, "Hello, it is a pleasure to finally meet you. Your husband talks about his family all the time."

Then I introduced them to LeRoy, who just kind of nodded his head. Ugh.

"Well," I said, "I hope you enjoy the show, I think we left the tickets in the car, so we're going back to get them."

Rodney said, "No problem. We'll save you a seat."

I could have hit him over the head.

As we walked towards the car, suddenly LeRoy said, "Ila, I have the tickets in my pocket."

So we turned around and Rodney was standing there waiting for us.

It was open seating, but since Rodney knew everyone, we were escorted to front row seats. The restaurant sat approximately one hundred people, but the tables were set in an intimate arrangement. We ordered hors d'oeuvres quickly. I felt if I got some food in LeRoy's stomach that maybe he would sober up a bit. The mushroom caps with cheese and sausage arrived, along with potato wedges cut in quarters filled with sour cream and bacon. That surely would stick to his stomach. We ordered a round of drinks and the lights went dim. Then out walked Boney James and his band. They were superb—two hours of non-stop jazz. I was in heaven. I made idle chit chat with Jackie and watched LeRoy move slowly down in his seat. I looked at Rodney who was laughing at us.

Minutes before the last set was over, I excused myself to go to the ladies room. Of course, Jackie felt that was her cue also. We walked through the tables and down the long hallway to the ladies room.

She said, "It's nice to finally put a face to the woman that my husband talks about everyday."

I didn't answer. We entered the ladies room and I was determined to finish before her and walk back alone. Dang, that didn't work either. It was a long walk back to the table. Fortunately, LeRoy was waiting at the front door. I said goodbye to Jackie and we walked very slowly to the car. It seemed that he had sobered up some, but as soon as we got in the car, he filled his ABC cup with Absolut. It was a cool evening and the moon was full. The "Quiet Storm" had gone off of WHUR, but they were still playing mellow music. I looked at his tapes and they were mainly gospel or books on tape. What was that about? Anyway, we were soon in front of my apartment. I started my goodnight spiel.

He said, "Start the car and pull into the parking lot beside your building."

I said, "Why?"

He said, "I have a surprise for you."

I thought about that for a minute. He was an executive at a bank and married. He had a lot to lose. I thought he was smart enough not to do anything stupid. I started the car, pulled into the dark parking lot, and parked the car. He instructed me to pull the seat all the way back and lay it flat. I thought, what kind of freak is he? Then from out of nowhere, he pulled out a towel.

"Please take your hose and panties off."

It was very quiet in the car as I did as he instructed. He placed the towel under my buttocks, lifted my dress, and proceeded to have oral sex for thirty minutes. Boy was I grateful. It had been a long time since I had had any kind of sex. I enjoyed the minutes of great pleasure. Once done, he took the bottle of Absolut, filled his mouth, swished it around, opened the door, and spit it out. I didn't know whether to be insulted or glad he was at least hygienic. As he pulled himself back into the car, he explained that after drinking as much as he had that night, getting an erection was out of the question. He wanted to do the next best thing. I thanked him. Then I picked up my panty hose, underwear, and shoes, and I opened the car door slowly. He walked to my side of the car. Yes, this was by far one of the strangest dates I had had in a long time. He thanked me for a great evening. I put on my heels and he walked me to the front door of my apartment. He told me he hoped that we could do this or something similar real soon. I told him I would call him when I got back from vacation. He nodded and left. As I climbed the steps, I knew that a shower and a long good night's sleep would make this night all seem like a dream. As I entered the door of my apartment, the phone was ringing.

I answered, "Hello."

Rodney said, "I just wanted to see if you got home okay."

I gave him the dial tone, took a shower, and went to bed.

I woke up around 10:00 a.m., jumped into a pair of sweats, sweatshirt, and tennis shoes. I put a scarf around my heard, picked up my keys and headed to the store for a paper, coffee, and then planned to pick up my cleaning—my Sunday routine. I had often wondered when I would get back to going to church on Sunday. I grew up going to church each Sunday. Somehow that tradition was lost when I moved to DC. I didn't know anyone who went to church on a regular basis. I think it was because we all worked on an average of ten to twelve hours a day, and some weekends. By the time Sunday came, we just wanted to thank God from our beds. Looking back on those days, I realize now that it was only by God's grace that I got through a lot of the situations I placed myself in. I walked slowly and enjoyed the morning. As I walked through the parking lot of the *7-Eleven*, I saw LeRoy's Audi. I looked inside the car and there he was asleep in the back seat. I decided to let him sleep it off and kept walking. As I left the store, my conscience got the best of me. I knocked on his car window, then the door, and the window again. Then I began calling his name. After many shouts and knocks later, he opened his eyes with a small grin. I gave him my coffee, croissant and paper, and told him to go home. I walked back into the store, refilled my order, ran to the cleaners, and strolled back to my apartment hoping to finish my packing without any incidents.

Of course, I had laundry to do and it was getting late. The laundry room had already begun to fill up. I hadn't heard from Paula and Drew this weekend, and I wondered if they were getting along. Maybe Paula had gone to her mother's house yet again. Unfortunately, I could not dwell on my neighbor's complex but loving relationship. As I came to the last flight of stairs, there sat Rodney. Didn't he like to spend his Sunday mornings at home?

"Hey," he said. "I wondered if you wanted to take a ride to Haines Point to see if your boy was there. You're going to be gone for some time and might need medication to take with you for the long and lonely nights. I smiled. He had read my mind, and I wondered how I was going to go on TDY for three months without any weed. I smiled, and told him I had not taken a shower, and was not ready for the public eye.

He said, "You won't even have to get out of the car if he's around."

He was right; it was a drive-up situation. Of course, I said, yes, and turned around to walk back down the steps. I was confused because I had not seen his car as I walked up the street.

I turned and said, "Where is your car?"

He said, "Oh, I guess you didn't find out. I'm going on TDY with you and they gave me a black Rivera so that we can blend in downtown and Southeast Washington."

I was stunned. I had to spend three months with masturbation boy. I began to laugh.

I said to him, "You will do anything to get out of your home. Your wife seems lovely and you have a young baby to be with. What are you doing going on TDY for three months?"

He said, "I needed surveillance duty credits and the other TDY for surveillance was in California. I felt it was better to get the credits here in DC so I wouldn't have to be that far away from my family. And, who else would let me masturbate every night without passing judgment?"

I could do nothing but laugh, while he opened the car door to this beautiful black-on-black Rivera. We cruised down I66 into the city and crossed the bridge to DC towards Haines Point. We had only been in the park about two minutes when we saw Hunter near the water. That was not his usual spot, so we were careful not to roll up on him. That was the signal that the police were somewhere in the area. We drove slowly past Hunter who didn't acknowledge us. He did get up and begin to walk along the rail of the water. Rodney drove around the bend, parked the car, and watched Hunter. He had a backpack on and I am sure it was filled with lids of weed. He slowly sat by a tree, left a bag at the base of the tree, and nodded his head. He stayed there for about ten minutes, got up, and began walking to the next tree. Since we were in a marked government car, it was better for us to get out, walk to the railing, and pretend to feed the ducks with my croissant while keeping an eye on the tree basin. If Hunter did this for us, he did it for his other clients, and we didn't want one of them to get our lid. We let some time pass, and then we walked over to the tree, sat down, and talked. We didn't know that this day would come back to haunt us. We thought that if the police were still around, they would have followed Hunter. But, we were wrong. After about an hour, we picked up the package and got into the car. It felt a little shaky, but we slowly drove out of the park without incident.

We traveled back to Virginia in silence; both thinking about what would happen if we got caught buying a lid of grass. As we crossed the state line into Virginia, we were feeling less scared. We stopped for more coffee and headed back to my apartment. I thought he would drop me off, but as soon as he parked, he jumped out of the car.

I said, "Have you packed?"

He replied, "Yes, I have been packing for the last week. I am supposed to pick you up in the morning, take you to security, get your assignment, and drive you to the location. I'll be staying in the same place, but in a different room or apartment."

He was not even sure where we were going for this assignment, but he knew for a while that he was accompanying me on this TDY.

We walked slowly into my apartment. He started telling me what he knew about the assignment and then decided we should take a walk. He said the walls were very thin. We walked to the metro stop and he explained the entire mission. I had to really rethink my wardrobe after that briefing. We walked back to the apartment and he walked to his car.

I said, "You're leaving?"

He said, "You're tired of me, I know."

I said, "Yes, I will be in three months, but right now I could use the company."

He turned around and followed me up the steps into my apartment. I didn't want to tell him that I had not had real sex in sometime and if he were up for it, I would not say no. I played it cool and took him down friendship lane for about two hours. We fired up joints, put Absolut in our cold coffee and he turned on the TV to watch basketball. I continued to pack and then I came out of my room and told him I was going to take a shower. I asked him if he wanted to join me. He sat on the couch and didn't respond. I turned and walked to the shower. I turned on the water and the radio, undressed, and got in the shower. I also had to wash my hair, so I placed the shampoo on the shelf inside the shower. I was in the shower about five minutes when I heard the door open. He pulled the curtain aside and there he was standing at attention with lust in his eyes. He stepped into the shower and I placed the shampoo in his hand. He slowly poured the shampoo into my hair and rotated his hand movements to get all of it. I had never had a man wash my hair. It was fantastic. He placed my head under the water to remove the shampoo. Once again, he put shampoo in my hair and placed just a little more pressure using his rotating hands. After a short while, he rinsed the shampoo out and put conditioner in my hair. Then he slowly combed the knots out of my hair. I could not believe that his penis would stay hard this entire time. After placing the conditioner in my hair, he turned me around, bent me over, and requested that I touch my toes. I did as he requested and he entered me from the back. It took my breath away, with the water on my back and his penis in my pussy—slow at first and then faster and faster. I screamed with pleasure. He pulled his penis out, rinsed my hair, grabbed a towel off the rack in the shower, turned the water off, dried me off, and held my hand as I got out of the shower. Then he led me into the bedroom.

He asked me to sit on the side of the bed. He checked the locks on the front door, picked up incense off the dining room table, looked for matches and lit the incense. He sauntered into the room, rolled another joint and we sat on the side of the bed and smoked it. He got up, stood in front of me and placed his penis in my mouth. I was all over it. I wondered if he was a freaky kind of guy, so I slowly took my middle finger and began to massage his anus area. He bent over, so that more pressure and more fingers could be placed into his ass. I licked and pulled on his penis while his hips rolled in slow motion. He then pulled out from my grasp, rolled me over on the bed, and entered me sideways. I was weak at this point. I could not believe I had not made love to this man before. I knew this day would change our relationship forever. It was a little sad. He was my friend, and now he was my lover—things would change. Forty-five minutes later, he left me limp in the bed. He went to the kitchen and poured a glass of Absolut. Then he put on his pants, went to his car to get a VHS porn tape, and finished himself off. WOW! I thought I could hang. I was so wrong. When I woke up, it was 4:00 a.m. Rodney was gone, but he left a note saying he would be back at 9:00 a.m. to pick me up.

I rolled over, set the alarm for 7:00 a.m. and fell into a deep sleep. When the alarm went off, it startled me. Last night seemed like a dream—a good dream and a nightmare at the same time. I showered, packed my toiletries, and the rest of my clothes. I made awful-tasting instant coffee and had toast. I dressed very casually and waited for the knock at the door.

Rodney arrived on time, and took my bags to his new Rivera. I ran over to the maintenance lady to prepay my rent for three months and asked her to pick up my mail. Of course, I gave her a $100.00 to make sure the mail would be picked up and that my apartment would be watched. She nodded and I left. I got into the Rivera and we headed down Arlington Boulevard. I was a little confused because we were supposed to go to security to get the assignment. Then it dawned on me; Rodney already had the assignment and was taking me to the safe house. I remained quiet for most of the ride.

Finally, Rodney said, "I have the courage to love you and see you at your convenience."

I didn't respond. I didn't know how to respond. Any answer would be wrong. Silence was the best answer.

We pulled up to the Watergate apartments. Rodney had a gate pass. He placed it into the slot, the wooden arm rolled up, and he slowly drove around the building to the backside. He parked the car in a numbered space and turned off the ignition.

"Welcome to your new home," he said.

I looked around at this massive building and waited for him to tell me what the assignment would be. We got out of the car to talk in the open air. He began telling me about the assignment. We were to live as husband and wife. We were real estate brokers and were looking to open our own office. He handed me the assignment package, which contained IDs, real estate certificates, a new driver's license, and social security card. Also enclosed were pictures of the ten men we were supposed to tail for the next three months. It gave brief bios on each and mentioned if any had visual characteristics, i.e., scars, hairlines, etc. Each man would know they were being surveyed, but they had to pick us up on the street. Our first assignment was Tuesday morning at the Air and Space Museum. The client would be there looking at the new exhibition and having lunch in the cafeteria.

We walked to the back service elevator with our luggage and went to the sixth floor. Our apartment was located near the staircase at the very end of the hallway. It was also two apartments down from the service elevator. This was for easy access and exits, no matter the situation.

Rodney already had the keys, so he slowly opened the door into a completely furnished apartment. It was absolutely gorgeous. It had a full wet bar—stocked; black and white kitchen, which included appliances and all of the accoutrements. The drinking glasses were etched black and white. The floor had black and white tiles and the dinette table was glass with black and white chairs. It had two bedrooms, which had bathrooms attached, and each bedroom was on opposite sides of the apartment. In the middle was a common living/dining room area, which had huge sliding glass doors that entered onto a large balcony. I walked out on the balcony to see why this apartment had been chosen and found that it had a panoramic view of the entire complex. Very smart. We wanted no surprises. I started to get a little nervous, but this was the opportunity I had been waiting for. Rodney wanted the bedroom to the left of the front door and I am sure that strategically there was some significance there. I headed towards the other bedroom and began to unpack. I was starting to get hungry, but remembered that Rodney was an excellent cook. This was going to be a great three months.

After unpacking all of my things, I decided to get something to eat from the kitchen and review the bios and pictures of the clients. Rodney soon joined me after hearing the clanking of dishes in the kitchen. I had made a huge tuna and fruit salad with small crackers and bacon bits. They had thought of everything, including foods that we both enjoyed. Hats off to the administrator who did their homework for our stay.

Our first client was Thomas. He had gone to Northwestern and MIT; he'd graduated in June and was doing an internship on Capitol Hill for his cover story. He was originally from Denver, Colorado, and came from a large family. He had three sisters and four brothers. His parents were still alive and he was dating a college professor from the University of the District of Columbia.

We were going to do surveillance, but we were also being surveyed. There were three other couples doing the same thing and it was up to us to pick them out while we were on assignment. That task would be really hard, but Rodney and I had decided that I would do most of the legwork, and he would hang back with a camera to take pictures of our surroundings to see if we could pick up the other teams. This was a challenge I was up to doing. We sat and chatted about what we were going to wear tomorrow so that we would not stand out. Rodney said he was wearing a black and white dashiki, black jeans and a baseball cap. He was going to keep the camera around his neck to look like a complete tourist. I decided I would corn row my hair, wear very little make up and place my hazel contacts in my eyes. I'd wear too-tight jeans, tennis shoes and a Washington Red Skin's T-shirt, no jewelry, and just lipstick. This was going to be hard on me. I was used to dressing everyday for work, wearing a full complement of make-up and Nine West pumps. But, for the next three months, that sense of fashion was out the window.

We put on sweats, wrapped our heads in the new handkerchief craze and took a walk around the buildings. We had to look like a couple with some sense of normal behavior. Since we both were into walking, this would keep us in shape. While you are on TDY, you can get out of shape because of lack of sleep, poor eating habits, and you become a fast food junkie because of the late nights and early morning surveillances.

The complex was much larger than I expected. It was approximately 3.5 miles around both complexes. When we returned, we needed showers. I went right and he went left as we entered the apartment. I washed my hair so that it would have just enough kink in it to cornrow. The shower had pulse-beating heads that came from three angles. I stayed in the shower until I began to wrinkle. As I exited the shower, I heard the phone ring. I knew that there was not supposed to be any communication until the end of our first surveillance. At that juncture, we would meet to discuss the client and hear his taped conversation about what tails he had picked up while out that day. After listening to each tape, we would hear if the client had actually picked us up. If not, we would follow the client again another day. In the meantime, another team would shadow him until our rotation for him came up again. If at the end of the week he had not picked up the appropriate number of surveillance teams, he would have to go through surveillance training again in California. If you are not successful in California, then you are asked to consider another line of work.

The answering machine came on and the voice said the safe house would be at Georgetown University in the audiovisual building. Our names would be at the guard desk. We would find out later that this would be our permanent de-briefing area for the next three months. The teams would all meet at the end of each day at approximately 1700 hours in separate areas of the building. We would listen to the tape of the client to see if he had picked us up. If he had, we would have to stay at the Watergate until the next client was ready for training. If he had not, we would get another chance within two days. The other teams would shadow him until it was our turn again.

After the recording went off, Rodney looked at me and said, "You realize this is my last assignment in Washington. I'm being transferred to California in March."

I replied, "Will your family be joining you?"

He replied, "Yes."

It was November. I sat in silence thinking about how this transfer would affect our relationship. Who would bring me coffee and croissants unexpectedly? Who would be at the job to watch my back? Who would I watch porn with and if he knew, why did he make love to me? I stood up and walked into my room.

He yelled, "Is that it? Is that all you have to say?"

I kept walking and silently closed the bedroom door.

I looked at the dresser to make sure I had everything laid out for Tuesday—a small two-way radio, large hoop earrings, a press-on "Cat in the Hat" tattoo, matches, cigarettes and gum. I had a very small pouch that would contain three cigarettes, a book of matches, lipstick, gum, a whistle, ten one-dollar bills, a tampon (just in case), three aspirins, three tissues and six cough drops. I would carry the small two-way in my sock on the side of my leg. My jeans were tight but were wide legged, so the radio would not be seen, and my socks, along with a strip of masking tape, would hold it in place. That reminded me that I had forgotten to shave my legs. Nothing like taking tape off of legs with hair. Ouch! I got back into the shower to shave my legs and again stayed longer than I should have. The three-way pulse water was so inviting. I carefully shaved my legs and underarms. I dried off in the shower with my washcloth—a habit I had picked up from Phoenix. He hated water on the floor of the bathroom. I opened the door and reached for the towel, only to see a dim light in the bedroom and candles being lit. I was not up for making love to Rodney. It was bad enough that my stomach would hurt, and my mind wouldn't focus after making love to him. He sat on the side of the bed with a can of whipped cream and a joint. I dropped the towel.

The alarm went off at 8:00 a.m. and I was alone. For some reason, he would never stay in the bed. I thought he must have gotten up to watch porn during the night. I jumped up and took another shower. I was glad everything was laid out. I would have hated to think about what I was going to wear. We were the lead team today, so we wanted to be at the Air and Space Museum when it opened at 10:00 a.m. I entered the kitchen and found coffee and croissants on the table. Rodney was nowhere to be found. I sat down to enjoy the coffee and croissant when the door opened. There he stood—tall, dark and sweaty. He had taken a walk/run. He said it took the edge off before starting a new assignment. The croissant had been placed on a heated stone. This place had everything. My apartment was going to look pretty shabby after living here for three months.

Rodney was in the shower and I finished reading the *Washington Post*. At precisely 9:15 a.m., Rodney appeared ready to go. He stood at the door while I went to the bedroom and collected my things. We walked to the metro in silence. We had spoken briefly about my entering the museum and just looking around until he spotted the client. He would beep my two-way on vibrate to let me know the client was in the area. I knew there was nothing to say. I knew that because of our time and in the space that we were in, this could never be a relationship. It could only be what it was right now—an intimate friendship.

We arrived downtown, exited the metro and ascended the long escalator to the mall. We walked in silence and then walked apart after reaching the carousel on the mall. He went right, and I went left. The museum had opened up already so I ascended the steps quickly. Once at the top of the steps, I stopped, sat on the steps to the far right, and just watched people while trying to smoke a cigarette. I stood in this spot until the cigarette was finished, which was approximately ten minutes. There was no sign of the client. I decided to enter the museum and I almost ran into the back of him. There he stood looking at a replica of Amelia Earhart's plane. I continued down the hall into the next artifact room. There were models with clothing for the time period, plane propellers, helmets, and other time period artifacts in the room. I waited to see if he was coming into this area, but after ten minutes, I decided to take the elevator downstairs to see if he had gone into the cafeteria. As I walked towards the elevator, he was walking towards me. I was hoping that he was on his way to the artifact room, but no, he was getting on the elevator. This was my chance.

I said, "Hello."

He greeted me with, "Hello."

I asked him if he had any matches. He said he had a lighter, but would be glad to let me have it for he had another lighter in the car. I took his lighter and thanked him. We entered the elevator at the same time and rode to the basement. As we exited the elevator, I saw Rodney sitting in the rear of the cafeteria having tea. I was glad to see him because it gave me a reason to thank the client again and walk in the opposite direction. Rodney waved his hand to motion me over to where he was sitting. Rodney got up and turned his chair around so that he would not be facing the direction that the client was sitting.

He asked, "Do you think he made you?"

I replied, "I really don't think so. He looked like he felt sorry for me."

We sat in silence for a few minutes, just people watching and listening to the many different languages that were being spoken in the cafeteria. There were times when I really felt like I was in another country. Washington, DC is so diverse. At any moment, you could hear Spanish, Italian, Arabic, Chinese, Japanese, English brogue, and more.

Our client was having a bowl of fruit and a cup of coffee. Knowing he was a smoker, it would not be long before he would go outside and have a cigarette. At that point, Rodney would take over tailing him. Rodney could not take pictures inside the Air and Space Museum, so he was going to tail him to get pictures of his activity. I would meet him at the hot dog stand on the corner of Constitution Avenue and Ninth Street at 3:00 p.m. I looked up and the client was on the move. We cleared our space and walked fast to the elevator so that we could ride up with him.

I said, "So we meet again."

The client just laughed, and then said, "Are you from here?"

I said, "No, my boyfriend and I are just here for the weekend. We really love the museums."

That was the end of the conversation. As we exited the elevator, he made a left toward the IMAX Theater. Dang! That was very unexpected. We made a right and went outside. We looked on the museum locator only to find out that the show in the IMAX Theater started in five minutes.

Rodney said, "I'll wait until it is just about to start and go in. I'll get a seat in the back row. That meant I had to entertain myself for an hour until the IMAX film was over. He said he would beep me on the two-way when they were exiting the building. At that very moment, I heard the shutter of a camera click several times. There were two men to the right of us who were pretending to take pictures of the area. However, they were actually taking pictures of Rodney and I. Rodney continued into the building, and I sat on a bench at the base of the steps. I pulled out my small notebook and noted everything they had on, their height, hair color, and approximate size of their shoes. They'd been caught. The two laughed liked they were old friends and walked up the steps of the museum. I was sure that was team one. I didn't know how many more were out today and following us, as we had followed the client. I pulled out yet another cigarette and pretended to smoke it. It really smelled foul, but it was a good cover for the tail. I finished the cigarette and took the two-and-one-half block walk to the Museum of National History, when the two-way buzzed. I guess the client didn't stay through the entire movie. I began walking back, but decided not to take the direct route. I went down Independence Avenue about one block. Then I turned back on a side street and came upon the Air and Space Museum from the back. I took a seat and called Rodney on the two-way. He didn't answer. So the best thing for me to do was sit and wait.

I sat there once again people watching when out of nowhere, there was LeRoy and another lady were headed my way. I could not believe it. He was supposed to be in Alexandria, Virginia. What was he doing downtown? Probably he was creeping on his wife. I knew I looked like someone else, but I was not taking a chance. I immediately got up and began walking fast down Ninth Street towards Pennsylvania Avenue. I decided then that this was a good time just to stop and see the Jefferson Memorial to kill some time. I didn't have a camera so I decided to stop at a stand get a paper and a magazine. It was going to be a long couple of hours. I found an empty bench, and once again, I took a seat. Empty benches were hard to find in DC because of the homelessness. It was beginning to get colder, but I was layered with clothing just in case I needed to make a quick change. I read the paper and the magazine but still had not heard from Rodney. Looking around, he was nowhere in sight. People kept coming and going off the bench. I even had to take pictures for families who were visiting. It is a very interesting dynamic. When a family is together on vacation, they will ask almost anyone to take pictures of their family. In the almost two hours that I sat there, I had a very expensive Nikon, Canon, a video recorder and a Kodak Quick Shot handed to me to take pictures of families. If I had been a dishonest person, I could have run off with that Nikon, and gotten rid of it very easily in the next block. "I have always depended upon the kindness of strangers." The quote is from some movie, I think, and every time someone hands me a camera, I think about that quote.

It was 3:00 p.m. and still no Rodney. I continued to sit, but my butt was getting sore. I did get up several times and walk around. It was approximately 3:15 p.m. when the two-way went off. I retrieved it from my ankle. Rodney was on the corner of Constitution and Ninth looking for me. I told him where I was and he said that he would be walking up Ninth Street and we would meet half way. I wanted to find out where he had been and if he had been seen. I began to walk and soon I saw him walking toward me. He was very handsome. There was something about him that made all the women turn around, even when he wore his African outfit.

He seemed disturbed. As we walked towards each other, he motioned for me to turn around and walk back the way I came. I did. I walked back to the bench that I was sitting at and he walked right past me. Behind him about 500 feet was a short blonde woman in blue jeans, and a jean coat with converse tennis shoes. Alongside her was a very tall brown-skinned man, who appeared to be of Hispanic descent. He wore black jeans, a black jean jacket and they both had cameras. They stopped for a second to take a picture and walked past me. Of course, I was writing everything down as to their descriptions. I believe that was team two. Great looking out, Rodney. I believe we did very well today. I waited for the two-way to go off and it did approximately thirty minutes after the couple had passed me. Rodney told me to meet him at the subway station near the carousel; the same one we got off on this morning. We wouldn't need any exercise tonight. Well, I probably wouldn't, but I wasn't sure before the night was out that Rodney would be lifting weights and doing crunches. I wish I had that kind of dedication to fitness.

We had to take the metro to Georgetown University to get our debriefing for the day. As we sat in the last pair of seats on the metro, Rodney removed his coat and laid it across both our laps.

He whispered, "Open your jeans."

I said, "No."

He said, "Then let me open them."

What a freak, I thought. He slowly reached over, unbuttoned by jeans, and put his hands down my pants. I just laid his fingers there, and felt them slowly moving in and out of my vagina. I was a mess. I came very quietly in the back car of the metro. He laughed, pulled his fingers out, and wiped them on my jeans. Then he laughed again. What a freak! I buttoned my jeans before we exited the metro. We only had to walk a block to Georgetown University. We were to enter room 106 and wait. As we entered the university, I went to the ladies room, and he went to the men's room—to wash his hands, of course. I didn't want to look like I had been tossed, so I washed my face, put on fresh lipstick, and tried to get the ends of my braids from sticking straight up. As I exited the bathroom, just to the right was room 106. I didn't wait for Rodney. I just entered the room. It was about 5:00 p.m. or 1700 hours. I turned on one of the lights and sat down. It looked like a small conference room. It had one small oval table and six chairs. The room didn't have a white board, or other appointments that would make it look like a conference room. There were two tablets on the table and two sharpened pencils.

I heard someone whisper, "Ila, Ila."

It was freaky. I got up, looked outside the conference room door, and told him to come on it. He laughed. He thought I was still in the bathroom.

Rodney entered the conference room laughing so hard his stomach started to hurt.

"I really hope no one saw me at the ladies room door whispering your name."

I just looked at him. Sometimes I think he did more than smoke marijuana the way he acted. I really knew that he was just silly and serious all at the same time. He was a Dr Jekyll and Mr. Hyde; or the Incredible Hulk.

"You don't want to see me angry."

I laughed to myself. We sat quietly. It was after 5:00 and the conference room was so quiet. We didn't want to talk because the room may have been bugged. We waited. At approximately 5:20, a young man entered the conference room.

He said, "Here is your tape and recorder. Please keep the recorder. You will need it for future assignment tapes."

Then he left. We waited a few minutes and began to laugh hysterically. This was something out of a James Bond movie. The young man was so serious. I guess he didn't know it was just a training exercise. After laughing for what seemed like a half-hour, I placed the tape in the recorder and pushed play.

The client began by saying that the museum was a very hard place to pick up a surveillance team because of so many different kinds of people. I could not believe he said that considering he could be sent absolutely anywhere in the world on assignment. I was not sure he would make it through surveillance training. After a thirty-minute dissertation about his day, he finally said he picked up a surveillance team—two men. Then he described what they had on, how tall they were, etc. Rodney and I shouted with excitement. We had not been noticed, which meant we could go on assignment again tomorrow. We had to listen to the entire tape to find out where we were going on Tuesday. At the end of the tape, a soft voice notified us that our assignment would be at the Tyson's Corner Mall, in Tyson's Corner, Virginia. The client would begin his day at Lord and Taylor at 10:00 a.m. I looked at Rodney. To get from DC to Tyson's Corner, Virginia in the morning rush hour was going to be long and dreadful. We had to go back to the Watergate and get a good night's sleep.

We collected the tape recorder and our things. Then we left the conference room and headed towards Wisconsin Avenue. It was a cool, crisp evening and we were famished. One of my favorite restaurants was Clyde's of Georgetown. They had the best crab cakes in DC. Okay, they have better crab cakes at the Inner Harbor in Maryland, but we were in DC, and I had a craving for crab cakes. It was about a half mile to "M" street and we had been walking all day. Of course, Rodney didn't bat an eye and wanted to walk and not take a cab.

We walked in silence.

Rodney finally said, "I have to call my wife."

I said, "You should."

We walked a little further and before getting to Clyde's we saw a telephone booth. They were becoming harder and harder to find. A new technology called the cell phone was on the horizon, and cell phone trials were taking place in Washington, DC and Chicago. It was just a matter of time before the phone booth would be ancient history. Rodney climbed into the booth and dialed the number. I stood outside people watching. It was getting to be the dating hour, so there were many couples out, holding hands and enjoying each other's company. My father told me never to trust a man who would hold your hand in public. I never really knew what he meant by that. He also told me that when a man wants a woman, nothing and no one could stop him from seeing her.

Growing up in Pittsburgh on a block where everyone was either related or very close friends, is something that I enjoyed. There was always someone to play jacks with or jump rope with. There was always someone outside until the streetlights came on. Then we had to be on our respective porches. We would scream across the street at each other. However, for all the joy of growing up in that neighborhood, there was some fear. The fellows would shoot craps in the alley behind my house. The heroin addicts would shoot up in the apartment building on the corner, and then sit on the sidewalk and give you a hard time on your way to the corner store. I had no fear because most of the bad guys were my cousins or very good friends of my father. I had a wall of protection around me by being a member of my family. So, I would skip right by the junkies and buy chips from the bar in the alley. My dad was a big shot and everyone respected him. Of course, I took full advantage of that fact. I skipped through the alley, went to the Italian restaurant unaccompanied, and I went to my uncle's barbershop which was off limits to all of the young girls. I would go anyway and get money from one of my uncles who were shooting dice behind the barbershop. Then I'd head up Hamilton Hill to my friend Connie's house. As I drifted in and out of yesterday, Rodney came out of the phone booth with a curious look on his face. I stared at him.

He just shook his head and said, "Ready?"

We walked in silence again. That must have been some conversation.

Clyde's was a great place. It had a long oak bar, plank flooring, original oil paintings, and the back bar had its vintage railroad posters. It had a comfortable atmosphere and I could feel a cold beer on the back of my throat before we sat down. I looked around and was amazed at how many people were hanging out on a Tuesday night. I had to remember that this was a college town and every night was Saturday night. Rodney finally loosened up. He ordered *a* St. Paulie Girl and I ordered a Rolling Rock. The waiter came back and I ordered crab cakes. Rodney ordered blackened catfish, dirty rice, and a salad. I didn't think he would like blackened catfish, but the more I was with him, the more I found out about him.

We were in a booth, so I decided to do to him what he did to me on the subway. I took off my shoe and crawled my foot up his leg to his crotch. I began messaging his balls. He didn't move away. He is so nasty. I felt his hardness on the bottom of my foot. He finally told me to stop and began to laugh. It was good to see those pearly whites. Whatever was said on the phone was now in the back of his mind. He resumed talking like someone who had taken a vow of silence and had not talked forever. I just sat, listened, and laughed. The food came and we wolfed it down like college students in between classes. I knew better than to wolf down my food. I would regret it about one hour later when gas filled my stomach, and I would release gas all the way back to the Watergate. Rodney laughed every time I did it. I was embarrassed. That was one fact that I wanted to remain a secret. We left the restaurant and walked to the metro. It was getting late and we had to get up very early. We hopped on the metro and were soon at our stop. We walked fast. I had to go to the bathroom, and Rodney wanted to lift weights before 11:00 p.m. He did it every night before 11:00, if possible.

We entered the apartment. I ran in my direction, and he walked his way. I went straight to the bathroom to relieve myself. Dang, I knew better. After what seemed like forever, I felt dirty. I jumped into the shower. This time I heard the door open. What could he possibly want tonight? I was so tired. I finished my shower, brushed my hair, and flossed my teeth. I was hoping that if I took long enough he would leave. No such luck. I entered the bedroom and he was sitting in the chair.

"Rodney," I said, "what could you possibly want tonight? You must be tired."

Rodney said, "Please lie on the bed and pleasure yourself."

WOW, he must be intuitive because that was exactly what I was going to do before I went to bed, but not in his presence. I blew my hair dry, pulled it back in a ponytail, pulled back the sheets, and began masturbating. It was something I learned to do very early in my life. I can't remember not masturbating at least two times a week. As I rolled my hips and moaned, I looked at Rodney. He was in a zone, masturbating. I saw the towel beside him and that was a good thing. In about fifteen minutes, I heard this growl and then a moan. It was all over. He wiped himself clean, placed the towel in the dirty hamper, walked toward my bed, turned off the light, got in the bed, and began to snore. All I could do was smile. I placed the pillow under my head and fell asleep immediately. As I dozed off, I hoped that Rodney had locked the door and checked all the windows. Knowing him, he not only did it once, he did it twice. Before I knew it, the alarm clock was ringing. It was 6:00 a.m.

Rodney was up. I could smell the coffee and the food being prepared. Damn, I could be married to this man. I entered the kitchen to find toast, sausage, and juice. Small bunches of grapes and cantaloupes were on a saucer. I sat down and ate much slower this time, since I had not given any thought as to what I was going to wear today. I decided to go very bare—no makeup, hair pulled back, eyebrow pencil only, and lipstick. I'd wear tight, tight jeans, a crop top, and a light jacket. We would be inside most of the day, so a heavy jacket was not called for. We had to drive to Tyson's Corner, so we would be in the car. We finished a refreshing breakfast, and placed our dishes into the dishwasher. I didn't have a dishwasher in my apartment, so this was a luxury that I could really get used to. Rodney had finished his breakfast, and was in the shower.

Rodney entered the living room in a black pinstriped suit, a white linen shirt, black shoes, and a black and silver cap. He went to the kitchen and picked up a coffee cup and a black notebook. I entered the living room looking like an orphan. The most expensive thing I had on was *New Balance* tennis shoes. I had my backpack, filled with a blouse change, shoes, a baseball cap, makeup, two-way radio, cigarettes, and candy. We were ready. It was 8:00 a.m. and it would take us two hours to get to Tyson's Corners.

We took Route 50 to Route 7. Route 50 was bumper to bumper for approximately forty-five minutes. We didn't talk much before an assignment. We did talk about the plan, however. He was going to enter *Lord and Taylor* and he would drop me off in the middle of the mall. I was to walk back towards Lord and Taylor until I saw the client or Rodney, and then I would pick the client up from there. If I didn't see them within an hour, I was to sit on a bench and wait. Finally, we arrived at Tyson's Corners. He dropped me off at Macys, which was the next major entrance next to Lord and Taylors. It was approximately 9:57 a.m. We were really cutting it close. I jumped out of the car and walked into *Macys*. I loved this store but I knew I didn't have time to look around. Nevertheless, this black and white checked jacket caught my eye. It was the new rage. I had so much black in my closet, it would be nice to have a jacket to change with pants and sleeveless black dresses. I walked over to the jacket, tried on a size fourteen really quickly and ran to the cash register. Rodney was going to kill me, but, this way, I could look like a real shopper. I walked very fast to the exit and then to the open mall area. I noticed a youth program that looked like it had just started. Little children were everywhere. I saw mothers' nursing, and strollers. I heard cries and mothers' screaming, "Stop, don't run. Get over here." I stopped for a minute, looked around at the regulated madhouse, and wondered if this was ever going to be me. Would I ever get the chance to nurse my child, scream for him/her to come back or smell baby powder on a baby's neck? A tear rolled down my cheek. I hadn't even realized how this moment had struck me. I wiped the tear from my eye and walked fast toward *Lord and Taylor*. As I got closer to *Foot Locker*, which was located right outside of *Lord and Taylor*, I took a seat on the bench.

I took a magazine out of my backpack and pretended like I was reading. I had been sitting for what felt like forever. The benches were not that comfortable. At approximately 10:45, the client entered the open area of the mall, but Rodney was nowhere to be seen. I kept my eye on the client as he walked past me, and slowly walked past each little store. At *Things Remembered*, he stopped to look at the small gifts they had in the window. Of course, I knew this was one way that he could look to see who passed him. He would try to focus on whether someone might be a tail. I stood back and just watched, but I didn't want to lose him in that sea of children.

I slowly got up and walked towards the *Naturalizer* shoe store. I also looked in the window, pretending to look at shoes. I was getting worried because I had not heard from Rodney. I would have to speak to our coordinator about the communication method Rodney and I had. The client was on the move and had walked through the sea of children. He kept walking towards *Hechts*. I decided to walk fast to get in front of him and have a seat on a bench. I walked quickly and sat on a bench outside of *Hechts*. Suddenly, he turned around and started back to the food court. Once again, I waited for him to get ahead of me and I followed. I had a feeling he had spotted me on the bench. As soon as he got something to eat, I would go into the bathroom and change my clothes. He walked extremely slowly. Then, all of sudden, he turned around and asked the blonde behind him if she had the time. She looked at her watch and gave him the time. I decided to hang further back. He walked to *McDonalds* and the blonde walked to a small coffee shop. She ordered a cup of coffee and a roll. I walked to the bathroom, changed my tennis shoes to low heels, turned up the cuff on my jeans, placed a blue blouse over my crop top, put on lipstick, and placed the baseball cap on my head. That took all of seven minutes. I walked quickly out of the bathroom and hoped that I had not lost the client and the blonde, who I felt was part of another surveillance team. I entered the long hallway from the bathroom only to see a young man talking into a two-way radio. He could have been mall security, but I was not taking any chances. I took a mental note of everything he had on, and ran over to *Wok and Wing*. I got a cup of coffee and took a seat.

They were both eating very slowly and looking around. They both looked past me. I knew I had not been made. They had no idea that a black woman was part of the surveillance team. For once, it was an advantage. I waited them out. I took out my notebook so I would not forget to write down what the blonde had on and what her partner was wearing. Just then, the blonde got up and walked toward *Nordstroms*. A second later, the young man took her seat. The client was still eating and trying not to look like he was canvassing the area. He finished his meal, sat for approximately ten more minutes, and was on the move again. I still had not heard from Rodney, and I was beginning to worry. The client moved, and seconds later, the young man moved. Seconds later, I moved. The client was walking towards the *Barnes and Noble* bookstore. I knew that that was a set-up. I would not be following him into the bookstore. They both entered the bookstore. I held back and slipped into a small restaurant next to the bookstore. I requested a booth that looked out into the open mall area. The only danger of staying put was that the bookstore was an anchor store and had many exits to the parking lot. I felt I should go with my gut and sit still. I wanted to hear from Rodney, but didn't want to pull my two-way out in the restaurant. I should have tried to reach him while I was in the bathroom.

All of a sudden, a man came out of nowhere and slipped into the booth where I was sitting. He looked me in the eye, laid keys down on the table, and said that Rodney's mother had had a heart attack. He had been taken to the Arlington Hospital. He said the car was parked where we left it and that there would be no communication from Rodney today. Then he left. Minutes later, the client exited the bookstore and was on the move again. This guy was on his job, not staying in one place too long. I waited to see if the young man would exit the bookstore. Sure enough, minutes later, he was on the move. I paid my bill and walked quickly into the open area of the mall. The client got onto the escalator and began riding and looking. I decided to take the steps. Thank God I had kept my walking regimen up. Out of breath, I waited for him to get off on the second level, but he didn't. He continued to the third level where the movie theater was. Dang, he was smart. I hung back and waited. The young man got off on the second floor. Soon the blonde appeared and took the next set of escalators to the movie theater level. I went back to the bathroom, and put my tennis shoes back on. I took off my baseball cap, took my hair out of the ponytail, tied the red shirt around my waist and put on my reading glasses. I put everything in my backpack, left the bathroom, and walked past the young man. I took the escalator to the theater level and saw them in line waiting to see a James Bond movie. Ugh. It was going to be a long afternoon. As I stood in line, the blonde looked at me slowly and I don't think it was a look of recognition—just a female look, like what does she have on. I laughed. I entered the movie and sat in the seat next to the last row at the top of the theater. I needed a bird nest seat. Halfway through the movie, the client was on the move and so was the blonde. It was getting late and I decided to finish watching the movie. Later, I would drive to Georgetown for the debriefing. I was worried about Rodney and I wondered if he would be pulled off the assignment. Perhaps he would request to be pulled off the assignment while his mother recuperated. The movie ended, I exited the theater, and walked to *Lord and Taylor* while dreading the drive back to Georgetown in traffic. At this point, I had nothing but time. It took approximately two hours. I arrived at the conference room at Georgetown at exactly 1700 hours. I went to the bathroom just to wash my face and hands. I exited the bathroom and walked slowly into the conference room. I turned on the light, took a seat, and waited. At 1720, a young man came in and placed a tape recorder on the table. He said nothing.

I said to him "is there any way Rodney and I can get pagers? These two-way radios are just not the type of equipment that should be used for surveillance."

He looked at me and nodded, but didn't answer the question. He requested that I leave my report on the table.

He also stated that I was not supposed to listen to the tape until my report was finished. Once I finished my report, I was to place it in the envelope he provided and leave it on the table. Then he left the room.

I took my notes out of the backpack and began to write my report. It took approximately forty minutes. I had more detail than I thought. However, I felt the more detail I wrote down, the better. Rodney would have written a shorter version. I began to laugh. Rodney would be walking around the room by now, waiting for me to finish so that we could listen to the tape. I completed the report and pushed play on the tape recorder. The client was very clear about his day and said that he had picked up the other surveillance team. However, he had not picked me up. I was good for another day. I left everything on the table and headed to the parking lot. It was late and I was starving. I wanted a fish sandwich from a small joint in Anacastia. It was not the best part of town, but this tiny storefront restaurant had the best fish. I drove to Southwest Parkway, and hopped off onto the Eleventh Street Bridge. I took the Anacostia Freeway to Anacostia Drive. Once at the restaurant, I ordered fries and a fish sandwich. It was piled high with fish, tartar sauce, cheese, and ketchup. The fries were so greasy that the bag was dripping in grease before I could get back to my car. I couldn't wait. I leaned the seat back, spread the heart attack meal on the passenger's side, placed the tall sweet tea on the dashboard and went to work. Of course, when it was over, all I could think about was the additional half-mile I would have to walk in the morning. I could feel the grease on my hands and around my mouth. Since I was alone, I just let it surround my mouth like a two-year-old child. It was fabulous. After the meal of death, I leaned back and felt its damage in my stomach. This was not something that I did all the time, but with Rodney not being at the apartment, I needed to kill some time. It would be difficult to sleep in the apartment knowing he would not be there. I sat for a few more minutes watching people come in and out of the restaurant. There was nothing like an all-Black environment. It always feels like home. Everyone greeted each other with a smile and words of greeting that included, "How is your mother?" or "How is your father, your sister, and grandma?" Anacostia was a tight knit community that was slowly being destroyed by a new drug called "crack." I didn't know much about it, but I understood that it was deadly and that one hit was enough to have you hooked for life. It was said to be cheap to buy and plentiful in this neighborhood. As I drove off, I prayed that it would not destroy a community where everyone knew each other and where church was the spiritual and social event of the week.

I slowly drove to the Watergate, and took in the wonder of downtown DC at night where the buildings were half lit, small crowds of people were still downtown enjoying the statutes, the memorials, and just the pomp and circumstance of being in the nation's capitol. I entered the parking lot and my legs turned to Jell-O. I had become extremely tired. It was after 11:00 p.m. and the day had been long. I walked quickly through the parking lot, into the building and up the elevator to the apartment. As I got closer to the door, I saw that there was a box on the floor in front of the door. I was not expecting a package, but I knew that the building was pretty secure. I wasn't afraid it might be something other than a package from the company. I bent down to get the package and wondered what it could be. There were no markings. I opened the door, and began to place the dead bolt on, when I thought maybe Rodney would come back tonight. I left the dead bolt off. I walked slowly to the bedroom, stripped quickly, and got into the shower after it had started to steam from the hot water. I stayed under the water until the water became almost cold. I then began to wash up. I washed my hair and conditioned it really well. I was going to wear it naturally for the surveillance tomorrow. I left the conditioner in and exited the shower. They had provided us with bath towels that felt like a warm terry cloth—huge nap and very large. I wondered if I could take the towels at the end of the assignment. I laughed hard. This picture came to my mind of me talking to my mother.

"Mom, I lost my job."

My mother would reply, "Why?"

Then I'd reply, "I stole towels."

After this flashed in my head, I decided the towels would stay.

I walked back into the living room to see what was in the box. I opened it slowly. Enclosed were pagers for Rodney and I, along with directions on their use. This would work much better than the two-way radios. I walked over to the phone to get my assignment for the next day. As I pushed the button, I noticed that there were several messages. The first message was about the assignment for the next day. The voice said that since my partner was not able to participate in the assignment, I would have the day off until they could find a replacement for my partner. The second message was from Rodney stating that he was okay and would be in touch. The third message was from the same voice as the first message. The man said that my new partner would be reporting to the apartment at 6:00 p.m. the next day. I was to be at the apartment so that introductions and assignments could be given. That meant I had the entire day to relax and maybe run to Virginia, and get my messages early in the day before everyone woke up. I could even get a newspaper, coffee, and a bagel. It is amazing how you miss the little things when you are on assignment.

I dragged my body into the bed and I fell into a very deep sleep. I left the lights and the TV on. I was thinking in my mind as I fell off to sleep, to get up, turn off the lights and the TV. None of that happened. I looked at the clock. It was

1:30 a.m. That was the last thing I remembered until I heard the front door open around 5:30 a.m. Rodney slipped into the room and into the bed. I was so glad to hear and feel him. He held me close, and I immediately wanted to know what had happened, how it had happened, and what was going on now. Before I could get out another word, he was between my legs. My moans could be heard, I am sure, in the next apartment. It was two hours of pleasure. The next thing I remember it was 12:00 noon and Rodney was gone. He had left a note on the dresser. I sat and read the small note.

"I will be back in one week. I just have to get my mother situated and I will be back. Love, Rodney."

I looked into the mirror and a tear rolled down my face. I would have to pull myself together. He was a married man. I was his partner and this was an assignment, not a lifelong commitment. I drew a hot bath. It was my intention to stay in the tub until my skin wrinkled. I lit candles, made a cup of coffee, and got the only book I brought by *Mary Higgins Clark*. I relaxed in the tub until the water got cold. I ran more hot water in the tub. I looked at the bedroom clock. It was 2:00 p.m. I had to get up and prepare myself for my new partner. I was hopeful that Rodney could get things together over the weekend, and I would only have to be with the new partner for one day.

I pulled myself out of the tub, and rubbed my body down with Vaseline, from head to toe. That was my beauty secret. I finally brushed my teeth, blew my hair dry, and placed it in a ponytail. I cleaned the bathroom and walked toward the dresser to pull out a pair of gray sweats and a gray top. That would be my attire for the day. I made up the bed and convinced myself not to lie back down because if I did, the new guy would be at the door and I would be asleep. I managed to make my way to the kitchen, and then all of a sudden, I was very hungry. I began preparing a salad. I turned on the oven so that I could place a chicken breast into a pan for the salad. Frozen chicken breasts were so convenient. I defrosted the chicken breast in the microwave, after reading the instructions, of course. This microwave would have me completely spoiled. I sprinkled lots of garlic powder and black pepper on the chicken breast and placed it in the oven. I pulled out romaine and iceberg lettuce, cucumbers, bacon bits, baby Swiss cheese and croutons. I put everything on a bed of lettuce, along with a sliced apple. I really don't know when they replenished the refrigerator, but whoever did it was doing a superb job. I waited approximately twenty minutes for the chicken breast to be done. Then I cut it up in small chunks and dripped low-fat ranch dressing on top of everything. I placed as many ice cubes as possible in a glass and opened a bottle of German Riesling. I placed it on ice to melt down the potency. I sat the plate on the table, along with the water glass of Riesling just as the doorbell rang. I thought it was too early for the new partner to arrive so I was timid about answering the door. First of all, the new partner should have had a key. I walked slowly to the door and looked through the peephole. The person on the other side was holding flowers. It was hard to see the person's face. I requested through the door what they wanted and the voice said he had a flower delivery. He must have made it through security at the front desk, so I opened the door. There stood Rodney, with flowers. I was elated to see him. I grabbed the flowers out of his hand, and pulled him into the apartment.

"What happened?" I asked.

He replied, "I convinced the company that replacing me could compromise the team since we worked so well together. I asked if they could just give us a new assignment for Monday." Rodney said, "They felt it was an appropriate request."

They told him to secure his personal business and then they handed him an envelope with the new assignment for Monday. I was elated. Rodney was hungry. He walked slowly to the kitchen table and sat down in front of my salad. He looked at me. I looked at him with a stern look, and he looked at the utensils on the counter. He nodded to me to get him a fork and knife. I obliged him, and he went to work on my salad. I went to work preparing another one.

He talked non-stop about his mother and the situation. She was coming out of the hospital in the morning. He had gotten in touch with the Virginia Visiting Nurses Association and had arranged for nurses to be at his home in twelve-hour shifts for the next two weeks. After that, they would see where they were. Rodney explained that his mother had great health insurance, but it only paid a portion of the nurse's salary. He would have to pick up extra details after this assignment to pay for everything. He also said he stopped by and got us tickets to see the Ramsey Lewis Trio at the Carter Baron and requested that I please change my clothes and do something with my hair after I finished my salad. He was very particular about how I looked when we were not on assignment. There were also certain things he didn't like me wearing—tight jeans, halter-tops, no back blouses, and very high heels. I have always been very conservative in my dress, so that was not a problem for me. The only time I took it to the extreme was while we were on assignment. Ramsey Lewis was due to go on stage at 7:00 p.m., so I cleaned up my area at the table, placed the dishes in the dishwasher, and went to my room to begin dressing. I looked through the closet, but there was not much to choose from. I had left most of my clothing in Virginia. I decided on a beige pair of slacks, a chocolate brown light sweater, brown clogs, and a heavy jacket. I plugged in my hot curlers and I heard the phone ring.

Rodney ran to the phone and all I heard was, "Okay. All right, okay. Yes, I will be right there."

Rodney walked into the bedroom and told me his mother had taken a turn for the worse. He handed me the tickets and he left. I looked at the tickets as he walked out the bedroom door. I wondered if I should go alone or call a friend. If I did call a friend, who would that be? We are in the business that we are in, and friends are few. I sat on the side of the bed and decided I would page LeRoy. I remembered he had a pager number on his business card. I paged him and left him the number at the security desk. I took the elevator to the security desk and told the officer that a man by the name of LeRoy would be calling me. I requested that the security man tell LeRoy to meet me outside the front gate at the Carter Baron if he was available at 7:00 p.m. The security officer said that he would, and I returned to the apartment. I continued getting dressed and made my way to the Carter Baron, hoping and not hoping that LeRoy would be there.

While driving, I thought how incredible it was that I could not find a single man in the entire metropolitan area. It dawned on me that I might not want a single man. I was secure in relationships that didn't require a complete commitment from me. I was always wearing my parachute. I was not going to take a leap of faith without a net. It was not in my nature.

I pulled into the parking lot and it took several minutes to find a parking space. I walked slowly to the entrance and there he was looking like fine vanilla chocolate. He had on a cream fitted sweater, long-sleeved, and cream linen pants with brown *Keds*. My, my, my, if he were only five shades darker. We walked in silence. He had been drinking and was not feeling any pain. He smiled a Colgate smile and reached down to kiss me on the cheek. We had tickets for the fourth row from the front. Only Rodney could score those kinds of tickets. He probably knew someone at the box office. Soon after we had our seat, a joint came down the row. It smelled very potent and I was tempted, but being on assignment, they can require a pee test at any time. I sniffed it and handed it to LeRoy. He dragged on it a long time and passed it back. Soon after, a local group, Chuck Brown and the Soul Searchers came on and rocked the house. It didn't take long for LeRoy to bring out his flask. He took a long swig and handed it to me. I took a long swig. It tasted like Remi Martin. I knew if I had hit that two more times, it would be over for me. Chuck Brown and the Soul Searchers ended and the DJ from WHUR, Donnie Simpson, came out on stage. All the women lost their minds. He was very handsome and had a great personality. I always felt he was more comfortable behind the radio mike than being in front of an audience. He gave us the rundown of the upcoming events, and he said that Envogue would be there in three weeks. I would be sure to ask Rodney to use his influence to get tickets to that show. LeRoy excused himself to the men's room, and I knew by the time he got back, he would be lit up like a Christmas tree. I just hoped I didn't have to drive him home again. He was gone a very long time. At first, I thought he might not come back. Ramsey Lewis had already taken the stage when he returned. I gave him a look like where have you been.

He said, "I ran into a colleague who wanted to come back to the seat and meet my wife. So I stayed and turned the conversation to business. Before I knew it, Ramsey was on and I told him he could meet my wife another time."

The concert was incredible. Ramsey Lewis and his trio played everything anyone would have wanted to hear. When he left the stage, there was no reason to call him back out. He had given it his all. LeRoy and I stayed in our seats. We knew it would take approximately fifteen minutes to clear the amphitheater. LeRoy wanted to know why he had not heard from me and why I had not returned his phone calls. I told him that I had been out of town and had not had time to check my messages. He pulled the flask back out and we sat in silence finishing off the Remi Martin. I could feel a gentle glow coming on my face and in the pit of my stomach. I was glad for the lag of time before I had to get on the road to drive back to the Watergate. We looked around and the security guard was coming to tell us to leave the theater. We stood up and walked slowly to the parking lot. This was always the part I dreaded about dates of any kind. What do we do now?

LeRoy said, "Let's go to the Safari Club in North East."

I had not been there in ages and I felt like dancing.

I replied, "I'll follow you."

It took us about twenty minutes to get to the Club. It was hard to find a place to park. The Club was crowded. We parked around the corner and walked. You had to be very careful because parking restrictions surrounded the club. We walked the block and it was good for me because it cleared my head a bit. You could hear the reggae music outside the door. I thought since it was Wednesday night, it would be less crowded. But, I must have had a brain freeze. This was DC, and every night was Friday night if that was what you wanted. We entered the Club and there was a $5.00 cover charge. They had a local reggae group appearing. LeRoy paid the cover charge, and grabbed my hand, as we slithered through the bodies on the dance floor to the bar. There was only a small section open at the end and it had one chair. LeRoy strolled down to the empty chair offered it to me and waved for the bartender. As the bartender approached, he began to smile.

He said, "It is so very nice to see you again."

I think that was truly his line, I had not been in this club for at least a year. I blushed because LeRoy gave me this look like, "Yea, a year, my ass." I laughed. I told the bartender it was nice to see him again also. He asked me if I wanted a fresh rum punch that had just been made.

I nodded and said, "Of course."

He laughed and asked LeRoy what he would be having. LeRoy was smart. He decided to stick to dark liquor and ordered a double Hennessy straight up. The dance floor stayed full and it was very warm in the club. The bartender returned with our drinks.

We clicked glasses and LeRoy said, "This is just the beginning."

I didn't know what that meant, but I acknowledged and turned my glass up. It didn't take long to start feeling extremely good. LeRoy was rubbing my back and he made sure I felt the bulge in his pants in my back. I turned around, took his hand, and led him onto the dance floor. It was a slow reggae song. Bodies were close and the heat was intense. I could feel my hair drawing up, but I didn't care. I was feeling good. LeRoy held me close and once again made sure I knew that he only needed a word from me and we would be in a hotel. I didn't want that to happen. As fine as he was, I was already committed to one married man. I didn't want one more. He kissed me on my neck and cupped by breast with one hand. Oh, shit! I backed up and told him I had to use the ladies room.

He laughed and said, "Okay."

I walked through the sea of bodies to the ladies room and quickly splashed water on my face. I pulled my hair back and braided it really quickly. It was extremely hot. I pulled myself together and walked back to the bar. He was on the dance floor with a very attractive Caribbean woman, and I was glad he decided to rub his hardness all over her. She seemed to be enjoying it. It was my way out. Thank you, Lord. When he returned to the bar, he could not keep his eyes off her. I was not mad; just a little disappointed that he was disrespecting me. Oh, who was I kidding I was out with a married man, who only wanted to make sure his night was not a complete waste of time—particularly for all the lies he would have to tell, about being out so late on a Wednesday night. I gave him his out. I told him I had an early meeting in the morning, and that I was ready to go, but if he wanted to stay and enjoy the rest of the evening, he could. He nodded and walked me to my car. He kissed me on my cheek and I think he ran all the way back to the club. I laughed, turned on WHUR, and made the long trip back to Virginia. I pondered what I would do the rest of the week, since the company gave me a mini holiday. I decided that I would take advantage of the indoor gym, pool, and sauna—all of which was located in the Watergate. As I entered the gates to the Watergate, Blue Magic came on the radio. I had to sit in the car until the song was over. What memories that brought up. I shook those thoughts out of my head and got out of the car.

As I entered the building, the security guard was waving a manila envelope. That could not be good news. I thanked him and placed it underneath my arm. Then I walked very slowly to the elevator. I didn't want the guard to know that it was only by God's grace that I drove back to the apartment and hadn't hurt myself or anyone else.

I entered the apartment, and saw the light flashing on the answering machine. That couldn't be good news. I plopped down on the couch, opened the envelope, and read the directions to a secure facility. An attached note told me to report to the facility at 10:00 a.m. tomorrow. I looked at the light blinking and knew I had to get the message. I dialed the secure number to retrieve the message. The message said that a white Ford Taurus would be parked in space 209 with the keys in it. I was instructed to take this car to the secure facility for my next assignment. I looked at the directions and was mad that I had to drive all the way to Sterling, Virginia for the next three or four days, depending upon how long the assignment would last.

I looked at the clock, got up, and placed myself in a long hot shower. Then I found the most business-like outfit I had and placed it on the chair, along with stockings, heels, and a business bag. I secured the apartment, called the security guard, and told him to call me at 7:00 a.m.

He laughed and said, "Why don't you set your alarm?"

I told him that I would, but he was my back up.

He laughed again and said, "Sure."

Making my way up Route 50 because I66 was still under construction was a trying experience. I decided to just be patient and make the best of a beautiful morning in DC. I had not heard from Rodney. I was hoping he would have called this morning. I had my pager on my hip just in case he got to page me later in the day. I had no idea what this assignment was about. I just knew that it would be an administrative nightmare, and that I would have to walk into it every day until Rodney returned to work. My only saving grace was I knew it would be temporary.

I turned into the parking lot of the Georgetown University Extension building, parked, and walked into the building. I headed to the elevators, got in, and pushed the button for the fifth floor. Little did I know, I couldn't go above the fifth floor. The elevators automatically stopped there. I had to exit the elevator on the fifth floor, be body scanned, badge scanned, and given a visitor's badge. I wondered if I would have to do this everyday. If so, it would be important for me to get up earlier. I laughed to myself, because getting up early, particularly when I was by myself, was very hard to do. I was passed through the body scan and badge scan and was told to take the elevator to the eighth floor and speak to the receptionist about where to go next. She would have my name and my assignment. Since this was an undercover building, I was sure that contacting my boss would be out of the question. I just wondered if he knew how long I would be required to stay on this assignment. Would I be here even after Rodney returned? Would they find him another partner? Those were questions I was not allowed to ask.

As my boss would always tell me, "Ila, do your job and keep your head low."

That is exactly what I was going to do on this assignment. I was surprised they didn't take my pager, but it was company issued so I guess it was authorized even before I got here.

I rode the elevator to the eighth floor, got off and walked to the reception desk. She greeted me by name and told me to walk down the hall, make the first left and enter the conference room. She told me someone would be with me shortly. I did as she requested and helped myself to fresh brewed coffee and fruit. After I had served myself, I hoped that it had been left there for me and not another meeting. Anyway, I was too late. The coffee was good and the fruit was fresh. In walked a very good-looking white man, with a yellow pad and a pencil. He had on Dockers and a striped shirt, but his manner was so cool. I didn't know if he was just shy cool, or cool, cool. Either way, he walked in with control and I liked a man who could walk in and control a room. He introduced himself as Dr. Raymond Zarnoff. He was a MIT graduate and needed help for a few days while his assistant was out with the flu. He wondered if I could be the one to get the job done. I told him a little about myself, and the positions I had held. He was impressed. He told me to follow him to his office. As we walked down the long corridors, small talk came easy. I felt this was not going to be as bad as I had thought. We arrived at his office that had a panoramic view, but his windows were tinted and his computer was in the middle of the room. That told me that he was working on top-secret material. Computers were not allowed near windows for fear of interception. We walked into his office and requested that I have a seat. He said he was working on satellite interception and that he needed a white paper to the Pentagon in two weeks. He also said he was a poor writer but a magnificent mathematician. It would be my responsibility to get all the spelling and grammar issues correct and he would worry about the formulas and equations. He said the text he would write in longhand because he did most of his writing at night. He couldn't seem to get into typing and thinking at the same time. He did say that all the formulas and equations would be done on the computer, so I would only have to cut and paste. At that moment, of course, my pager went off. His facial expression told me he didn't approve. I looked at the number, and turned it on vibrate.

He said, "I do not want to hear that pager go off again."

I replied, "Don't worry. It won't happen again."

Those were the only stern words he said to me during the entire assignment.

We spoke about his routine, and how he wanted to go over his daily calendar every evening before I went home— even if he was busy. He also said he was a late riser, so I would not have to arrive at work until 10:00 a.m., but I had to work until 8:00 p.m. or later. I tried to contain myself because those hours were perfect for me. I wondered how I could keep this job. I smiled to myself. He got up, and wandered over to a door that I thought was his bathroom. Instead, it was an office for me. Off of that office was a conference room and a small kitchenette. He said that the refrigerator would always be stocked with water, juice, and fruit. He only ate twice a day and that was breakfast and a light dinner. In other words, there would be no lunch for either of us. We would be working through lunch. Since I didn't have to be at work until 10:00 a.m. that sounded reasonable to me. I wondered if I had to walk through his office everyday, but then I noticed a door behind my desk and one off of the conference room. He told me to familiarize myself with the desk and the floor. He would use the intercom system if he needed my assistance. I was told to check his outbox every hour for text, just in case he had moments of greatness. We both laughed. He did say that there was text currently in the box from last night and requested that I retrieve it and start placing it into white paper format. His assistant had not begun the paper, so I was starting from scratch. He also requested that I go back to security on the fifth floor to receive the combination to the safes, and keys to the offices, the conference room, and whatever else required by security. He would call human resources and tell them I was going to stay through the assignment.

He was talking and all I wanted to do was use the phone, but I didn't have the code of a secure outside line. It would have to wait until I returned from security. I did as he said and became familiar with my surroundings. I met some of the other ladies that worked there. I was not trying to make friends since this was a temporary assignment. I found the ladies room, the cafeteria, the gym, and security. The guys in security could not have been nicer. Everything went really smoothly. I got access codes, safe combinations, an interoffice phone book, and a key pass to the gym, and a phone number of one of the guards. It was going to be a great day.

I returned to the office to find Dr. Zarnoff sitting at the desk. I wondered if I had been gone too long. I had not wasted time; it just took a long time. I walked up to the desk and asked him how I could help him.

He replied, "I need to go home and write a section of the paper. I was hoping that you could come with me so that as I finish a page, you could type it into the computer."

He wanted me to drive him home and bring him back. Hmmmm, okay. I was game. He had a top-secret clearance and a reputation to uphold. I really didn't care where we did the work.

He said, "Okay, then, let me gather my things."

He did and we walked out to the back of the building. He placed his key card into the elevator slot and the door opened. We stepped into the elevator and he stepped into the other side, placed his key card in again, and the door on the other side opened up to a parking lot. His car was in the secure parking lot. He drove a black BMW sedan. It was extremely clean inside and out. He handed me the keys, gave me directions, and he got in the back seat. I proceeded to the driver's side and drove him to Centreville, Virginia.

It took us approximately twenty minutes to get to his home because of traffic. I turned into the driveway of a three-story colonial home with a wrap-around porch. The yard was fenced completely. It looked like a home for a married family with three or four children. The grounds were immaculate and the flowerbeds were flawless. I got out of the car, opened the back door, and shook him to wake him up. He woke looking dazed and got out of the car. We entered the house from the back. He said he never uses the front door and he never parks his car in the garage. Then I wondered how he keeps his car so clean. That question would be answered in a few short days.

We entered the house from the back, through a glassed-in porch. He had a surround sound stereo system, gray leather furniture, gray lamps, and black scatter rugs. It felt kind of cold, but warm at the same time. In the corner of this room were a desk, a computer, file cabinet, telephone, wastebasket, headphones, and a stack of floppy discs. I knew that this area was going to be my world. I laid my purse and the long handwritten pages on the desk. He had gone into the front part of the house. I felt since time was moving on that I should get started on the paper. I turned on the computer, only to find it had a password. I called out to Dr. Zarnoff, but got no answer.

I began to walk into the house when he bellowed, "Take off your shoes."

I did as I was told, but was not happy. I had on panty hose, probably the only pair I had. Then he yelled, and told me there were slippers in the closet to my left. I opened the closet and sure enough, there was a basket of slippers. I chose a red pair of slippers and instantly thought about how many people had had their feet in the flip-flops. I shook that thought away, and slowly entered the front of the house. I was surprised to see that it was sparsely furnished and it was all shades of gray, black, and brown. I am sure there was a story behind the décor, but I was also not sure I wanted to know the story. As I looked around, I heard water running. I could not believe he was taking a shower. What was that about? I yelled to him to tell me the password for the computer.

He yelled, "Wait until I get out of the shower."

I immediately turned around and headed back to the porch. I sat waiting patiently. After about twenty minutes, I walked back into the house only to find him asleep on the couch. I walked over and shook him awake. He sure did sleep a lot. He again looked at me with glazed eyes. He got up, walked to the porch, went to the computer, and typed in the password. Then he went back into the house. I took a seat at the computer and began typing the white paper. His handwriting was hard to read, but once I got used to the "r" and the "t" looking alike, it was not so hard. The formulas I had become familiar with when I worked for the gentleman who helped to build the Alaskan Gas Pipeline. However, that is another story.

It was beginning to get dark and I looked at the clock on the computer only to see that it was approximately 1930. I had not returned the page and it had gone off several more times since I had entered the house. I knew it was Rodney and I was busting at the seams to speak to him. I saved what I had typed to a floppy disc and placed it in an envelope marked SECRET. I was not sure how SECRET it was, but I would take it back to the office and lock it up in the safe. I walked back into the house, only to find him hard at work in an office off the kitchen. He had on loud music, which sounded like some kind of fusion jazz. It would not be long until I was introduced to the music of Miles Davis and Thelonious Monk. They were his favorite artists.

I interrupted his train of thought to let him know that the hour was getting late and we must return to the building.

He looked at his watch and said. "You take these pages with you tonight. Take my car and pick me up in the morning at 0930 a.m."

I explained to him that I didn't have a secure place to leave the papers.

He said, "Oh no, stop by the office and secure the disc and the papers, and then go home."

I nodded and retrieved the keys from the desk on the porch and left him for the evening.

I could not wait to get home to answer my page. I went back to the office and placed everything in a secure safe. Driving his BMW was great; with WHUR spinning the smooth sounds of the "Quiet Storm," driving this vehicle could become a habit. It was a cool evening so I decided to let the sunroof back to see the starry night. It was a very pleasant ride back to the Watergate. I was about to enter the parking lot when I remembered that my pass was in my car. I pushed the button at the gate and had to explain to the guard that answered the page that I left my pass in my car. I told him that I was driving my boss's car and needed to be pressed in. We went through the drill of which apartment I was staying in, how long I'd been in the apartment and whose name was on the lease. After answering those questions, he buzzed the gate. I would remember next time to make sure I got my pass card. I had a feeling this would not be the last time I drove this car.

I entered the apartment exhausted. It had been an interesting day. This assignment was not going to be as hard as I thought and the doctor was a nice enough man. The telephone answering machine light was blinking and I hesitated to push the button. I decided to take off my clothes, take a shower, masturbate, and then push the button. I went to the refrigerator and found that it had been restocked and a new bottle of German Resiling had been placed in the refrigerator. I immediately opened the Resiling, and poured myself a healthy glass. I walked slowly into the bedroom and my pager went off again. It was a number I didn't recognize, but I knew Rodney was probably trying to get in touch. I walked back to the living room and pushed the button.

The voice said, "Hi, Ila, this is me. Sorry you have not heard from me, but it has been very hectic. My mom passed this morning. I have almost completed all the arrangements, but I still have a few more things to do in the morning. We are going to have her funeral on Friday at 10:00 a.m. I sure would love you to be there, but I heard you have a new assignment. You probably won't be able to make it. I love and miss you.

I quickly put in the code for unsecured access to the telephone and called the number on my pager, but there was no answer. I got up to go into the bedroom one more time, when I heard a key being pushed into the door. It could only be Rodney. I was so very glad to see him. I walked over, hugged him deeply, and handed him my glass of wine. I placed the inside lock on the door and walked slowly to the bedroom, removing clothes as I walked. He walked behind me and waited until I was completely naked to hug me tight. I could feel his hardness. I walked over to the shower, turned it on, and watched him disrobe. He was a beautiful specimen of a man. I could hardly contain myself. I walked into the shower and waited for him to join me. As he entered the shower, I slowly placed the washcloth on his back and rubbed him all over. I requested that he turn around so that I could wash the front of him. He had an erection and I dropped to my knees. I began slowly sucking the circumference of his penis. I placed my hand on his testicles and cupped them while placing his penis in my mouth with long inviting strokes. It didn't take long for the strokes to become more intense. I could feel him about to come. I opened wide and let the juice of his soul come into my mouth, and roll down the front of my face. I had missed him so much. I wanted to let him know. He lay on the back of the shower letting the water just run down the front of his body. I got up from the shower floor and began to lather myself up. I turned to look into his eyes and he began to cry. We stood there in each other's arms for what seemed like forever—just holding each other as the water drenched our very souls. I could see my fingers beginning to wrinkle. I told him to come out of the shower, finish his drink, and I would give him a long massage.

He said, "I only came by to hold you. I must go."

At that point, I began to cry, I needed to be held tonight. He slowly left the shower and walked into the bedroom. He picked up his glass of wine and began to take baby sips. Then all of a sudden he threw the glass back and drank all of it. He turned to look at me. I was toweling off and doing my nightly ritual of Vaseline and lotion. He walked over as I sat on the side of the bed, bent to his knees, and placed his hands between my thighs. Before I could say, "No, you have to go," I was calling his name, and I had his head in a thigh vice. He was laughing and eating me at the same time. After approximately thirty minutes. I asked him to stop, because I could not stand it anymore. He pushed me back into the bed. Then he placed a kiss on my forehead, pulled the covers over me, and set the alarm clock for 7:00 a.m. He put on his clothes, turned off the lights and left. I woke up when the alarm went off the next day.

I awoke to pouring rain. I wanted to walk around the complex, but knew that the rain sounded and looked like it was not going away. I slowly went through the apartment and picked up my clothes from the night before. It seemed like a dream. I had placed my pager on vibrate and had lain it on the dresser. It began to go off. I looked at the number, and it didn't look familiar. I didn't know if I should call back on a secure or unsecured line. I decided to be cautious and called it back on a secure line. The phone on the other end rang about five times. I figured whoever it was had decided to not talk.

On the sixth ring, a man's voice said, "Hello."

I replied, "Hi, I am answering a page to this number."

The person on the other end said, "Good morning, this is Dr. Zarnoff. I just wondered if you were up and getting yourself together to come pick me up."

I replied, "I thought you said 0930 a.m."

He said, "I did. I was just checking."

We made small talk. I asked him if we would be working at his home or at the office today. He said we would do one-half day at the office and one-half day at his home. I told him that I would see him at 0930.

He hesitated a minute, and said, "Okay."

I didn't know what the hesitation was about, but I am sure he had something to say to me and he'd say it at the proper time.

I took another shower, ran the blow dryer through my hair, pulled it back into a ponytail, and put on my makeup. I had decided to wear black slacks, and a lightweight white jacket. I was running out of outfits for work. I would have to get permission to return to my apartment for more clothes. While we were on surveillance duty, a lot of clothes were not necessary.

I grabbed the only umbrella in the apartment and headed downstairs to ride in the BMW once again. The rain had let up slightly, so the umbrella was just an extra precaution.

The traffic was terrible. I had left the apartment at approximately 0810 and that would give me plenty of time to get to Virginia before 0930. After what seemed forever, I drove into the driveway only to see a dark green Jetta parked very close to the steps. I hesitated a minute before getting out of the car. He probably had company and I was early. It was only 0905. I decided that he knew I was coming so what was the harm. I got out of the car, trying to make a lot of noise, but no one came out of the house. I knocked on the back porch door, but no one answered. The door was unlocked, so I let myself in and continued to the main part of the house. As I entered the living room area, Dr. Zarnoff had a young man bent over the couch and had penetrated him from behind. He was about to reach a climax. I turned around, and went back to the porch and waited. After about ten minutes, there was silence and good-byes were being said. The young man walked out to the porch and was startled to see me. I introduced myself to him. He said his name was Calvin. I told Calvin that I would move Dr. Zarnoff's BMW so that he could get out. He thanked me and we both left the house. I moved the BMW and the Jetta sped off. As I re-entered the house, Dr. Zarnoff came from the living room and asked me if I was ready to go. I told him I was ready. He never mentioned the young man and neither did I. We got to the office around 1000 and began working right away. I began typing the pages that he gave me last night and he reviewed what I had already done. Before I knew it, it was lunchtime. My pager had gone off earlier and of course, I wanted to call Rodney back as soon as possible. I went into Dr. Zarnoff's office to see if he wanted something from the cafeteria or if he wanted something from the deli down the street. He chose the deli down the street. I wrote down his order and left the building. It had stopped raining, so it was a very pleasant walk to the deli. I looked desperately for a pay phone. So many phones had been taken out of the streets because drug dealers were using them as their personal phones. As I entered the deli, I saw a pay phone. I placed our orders and immediately returned the page. Rodney answered the phone. He said things were going well and smooth. He would try to come by tonight if the family left early. If not, I would see him on the weekend. I could only shake my head.

He said, "Are you there?"

I said, "Yes."

He replied, "I will see you soon."

I said, "I know, I am counting on it."

He hung up the phone.

I retrieved the order and walked back to the office. It had begun to sprinkle and I hadn't brought my umbrella, but I was spared, as I walked into the office door, it poured. I went through the elevator, did the badge thing and walked slowly to the office. A few people who knew my name spoke, but I was walking in a fog. For some reason, darkness came into my spirit, I didn't know where it had come from, but it consumed me for the rest of the afternoon. The good thing about it was, I completed all of my work, and Dr. Zarnoff was ready to leave the office at 1800 hours. He once again requested that I drive him home. I told him that I could do it one more night but on Friday, I had to get my own car.

He laughed and said "Okay."

We rode in silence and listened to Herbie Hancock and George Benson. I was tickled that this White man from MIT loved this music. As we pulled into the driveway, he looked at me.

He said, "You met Calvin."

I said, "Yes."

He said, "No one knows."

I said, "Knows what?"

He looked at me, smiled, and got out of the car.

"Okay, 0930, right?"

I replied, "Yes, 0930 and not a minute sooner."

He smiled and walked into the house.

As I drove back to DC, the feeling of darkness came upon me again. It was like I had a feeling something was going to happen, but I wasn't sure what. I decided to stop into the WC Bone to see if they had any jazz for happy hour. As I entered the parking lot, I saw LeRoy's car. Damn, what was he doing in DC? I parked, looked in the mirror, put on lipstick, took my hair out of the ponytail, brushed it, and got out of the car. As I walked toward the entrance, I heard someone call my name. It was my friend, Sheila. I had not seen her since I went on TDY.

"Girl, where have you been?" she asked.

I told her I had been out of town on business and I thought I would stop to see if she was there. Of course, that was a lie, but it worked. She laughed and said she was going to change her hang out spot, if people were starting to look for her here. We both laughed and entered the building. LeRoy was at the bar with a young lady. I was hoping it was his wife. Then he wouldn't be compelled to come and say hello to me.

Sheila and I found good seats close to the jazz combo that was performing. It was a local group from Howard University and they were great. We sat through the set before getting drinks and food. As I walked up to the bar, LeRoy looked up and our eyes locked. He didn't make a move, so I knew that was his wife. Yea! I ordered Hennessy for me, and gin and tonic for Sheila. I went to pay for the drinks but the bartender said they had been taken care of. I nodded at LeRoy as I walked back to my seat. Sheila had gotten a pile of finger food from the complimentary bar and was going to work on it when I returned to the table. I marveled at Sheila. She was 130 pounds soaking wet and could eat like a truck driver. Me, everything I ate had a price and a place on my butt or my stomach. I laughed to myself as I joined her. The trio came out for the next set and drinks arrived at the table. Sheila asked the waitress where the drinks came from.

The waitress replied, "A benefactor."

Sheila laughed and said, "Hail to the benefactor."

We talked and enjoyed each other's company. It had been some time since we had hung out together. Sheila was in a relationship with an alcoholic DC police officer and she had a daughter, China, by the officer. Oh, did I mention he was married? There was so much of that going on in the nation's capitol.

It was 2200 hours and I needed to get up early. I told Sheila goodnight. She was waiting for Russell to get off his shift, and would meet her there. I asked her if she would be all right.

She replied, "Yes, but I sure wished I knew who the benefactor was."

I said, "Don't worry about it. The next drink is on me." I hugged her and walked up to the bar to order and pay for her gin and tonic. As the bartender walked back and laid the drink on the bar, once again he said it was paid for. I looked up and didn't see LeRoy, but I had a feeling he could see me. I thanked the bartender, and walked the drink over to Sheila. As I placed the drink on the table, Russell walked up. I kissed him on the cheek and told him it was getting late and that I had to run.

I walked slowly through the sea of people only to see LeRoy standing at the front door. He never said a word but walked alongside me until we reached the BMW.

His first words were, "New boyfriend?"

I replied, "No, new boss."

He said, "Yea right, call me Joe bologna head."

I laughed and said, "Okay, you are not going to believe the truth, so."

He looked at me and said, "You know with us, there has been nothing ventured and nothing gained. How can I break that cycle?"

I opened the door of the car, got in, started the engine, rolled down the window, and said, "Get a divorce."

He laughed as I drove away. It had begun to rain again, very hard, but I was not far from the Watergate so the drive was not that bad. Once again, I had forgotten my pass. I went through the gate and met up with the guard again. He told me that this would be he last time he would let me in without a pass. I thanked him and drove into the parking lot. I thought I saw Rodney's car, but I was sure he was still tied up with family. I walked slowly down the corridor to the apartment. I was tired all of a sudden. As I placed my key in the door, I could hear music. I knew it was Rodney. I immediately opened and closed the door, and applied the security lock. Rodney was in the bedroom fast asleep. I smiled, took a shower, and entered the bed. I cuffed myself around him. He never woke up. The alarm went off at 0600. Rodney must have set the clock.

Rodney rose fast, got in the shower, and was completely dressed before I could barely get my eyes open. As I struggled to start the day, Rodney was in the kitchen cooking and I could smell coffee. That was enough to get my body moving. I jumped up and got into the shower. I didn't take a lengthy shower because I was hoping that I would have to take another one in thirty minutes. I dried off and put on my sweat pants and a t-shirt. I walked slowly to the kitchen to savor the coffee smell. Rodney was sitting at the kitchen table with a large manila envelope. He looked very serious. I walked over and began to rub his neck. He bent into it but immediately requested that I sit down. I did, and looked into his eyes. Something was very wrong.

He said, "Ila, open up the envelope."

I did as he requested, and there we were at Haynes Point buying weed. Unfortunately, that day the DEA had a sting in the park and took pictures of everyone and everything.

I looked at Rodney and said, "Okay, so what now?"

He said, "I am being transferred to California and you will stay in the position in Sterling, Virginia with Dr. Zarnoff."

"Effective when?" I asked.

"Monday morning," he replied.

I was stunned, but the truth of the matter was that we could have been fired. A single tear fell from my eye. I knew this was the end of our relationship.

"How long will you be in California?"

"Five years," he replied.

"So that means your family is going TDY with you?"

"Yes," he replied.

I looked at the clock. Time was ticking away and I had to pick up Dr. Zarnoff. I walked to the sink to prepare a cup of coffee. He came up behind me, pulled down my sweat pants, and caressed my back down to the inside of my legs. I went limp almost immediately. He only had to touch me and my mind and body seemed to collapse. I knew that after this weekend, our relationship would come to and end.

I decided that I needed it rough, so I bent down and touched my toes as he entered me from behind, thrusting so hard I almost fell over. It was quick, powerful, and final. I cried heavily the entire time. After his climax, he walked over to the couch and summoned me to come to him. He laid me down and proceeded to have oral sex. He deeply thrust his tongue into my vagina, while placing his index finger up my ass. I was in another world. Then he suddenly stopped, got up, and walked out the door. I knew he would return tonight, but right now, it was too emotional for him to handle.

I again went to the sink to make a cup of coffee. After standing there for what seemed forever, I was glad I had gotten my wish. I entered the shower again, but it was not the shower I was expected to have. I got dressed slowly and still could not believe how our lives were going to change for one moment of insanity on our parts.

"WEED! My God, what were we thinking?"

I had to shake it off and get to work. I slowly walked to the corridor, and went down the elevator to the BMW. It seemed that it took forever to get to Dr. Zarnoff's home.

Again, Calvin was there, but he was having coffee. I walked in and screamed to Dr. Zarnoff that I was waiting for him.

I greeted Calvin, who immediately said, "Hi, Ila. Got to go."

Before I knew it, Calvin was out the door, and of course, I was blocking him in, so I went out to move the car. We said polite goodbyes and I walked back into the house. Dr. Zarnoff came to the porch with his hair dripping from the shower. He wore tennis shoes, kaki pants, and a white button down shirt. I thought, only in America could someone be so smart, so ill dressed, so gay, and one of the celebrated minds of the twentieth century. I just began to laugh. He looked at me and shook his head.

"Ready to go?" he asked.

I replied, "Yes, sir."

We drove to Sterling in silence. He didn't want to know that there was something wrong. He made it very clear on the first day, that my personal life was just that—personal. He didn't want it to interfere with the work we had to do, so therefore, his knowing was not important.

We arrived at the office, and I immediately gave him his keys.

I said, "Thank you for the elegant ride, but I must remember that I drive a Ford. I can't lose sight of that."

He laughed, took the keys, and proceeded to the front door. He loved to walk and talk, particularly outside because he always felt that people couldn't extract words from the air.

He was forever telling me, "Ila, let's take a walk."

I was scared somehow he would find out about the pictures, but he had not said anything. I was not about to give him any information. We went through the normal steps—elevator opening, everyone showing their badge and continuing to the upper floors.

The day was uneventful. He wrote, and I typed. He fell asleep; I woke him up to see what he wanted for lunch. Same thing—tuna on wheat, ends cut off, a whole tomato and a Dr. Pepper. Then he would walk for thirty minutes, come back to the office and work like a robot. Before I knew it, it was 1800, and the building was quiet. It was Friday, so most people left early. I went into his office only to find him stargazing with his telescope.

"Dr. Zarnoff," I said. "It is about time to go home."

He replied, "Oh, get the keys. I'm ready."

I replied, "Oh, no, not today. It's Friday. I'm going home."

He said, "Oh, okay. Take me home in your car and pick me up on Monday."

I replied, "What will you do for transportation over the weekend?"

He looked at me and winked.

"Oh," I said, "okay. Well, get ready."

I knew it would take him another twenty minutes to shut down, so I went back to my area, shut down the computers, took out the disc, locked it in the safe, placed some papers in the document shredder bag, cleared my desk, placed my phone on secure, and went to the ladies room. When I returned, he was sitting at my desk ready to go. We left and it had begun to snow. It was a freaky snow—coming down hard, but the snow was soft and fluffy. It was a long ride to his home. The snow started and stopped most of the trip. Once at his home he requested that I spend the night, but I told him I wanted to get home. He got out of the car and proceeded into the house. I turned around gingerly, and drove slowly back to DC. What usually took forty-five minutes, took almost two hours. I was so glad to see the Watergate. I had all my necessary credentials and sailed through the gate. I was hoping that Rodney's car would be there. No luck. I walked down the corridor slowly. All of a sudden, I was very tired. I opened the door slowly only to find my bags packed, the refrigerator emptied, and the apartment had been cleaned. There was an envelope on the table. I opened it. Enclosed were my orders to report to Dr. Zarnoff's office on Monday, and report to personnel on Wednesday for debriefing. I walked the apartment to make sure they had not missed anything. Of course, they hadn't. I left the keys to the apartment on the table, picked up my belongings, and left the apartment. As I walked past security, he handed me an envelope. I thanked him and walked to my car. I finally broke down and cried. This was going to change everything. The reality of the situation was that Rodney was and is a married man. I should be thanking God for my job and moving on. I wiped my eyes, placed the keys in the ignition, and drove slowly back to Arlington.

The weekend was uneventful. I went to the post office on Saturday morning to get my mail that had been building up for weeks. I went to my favorite bagel place, got coffee and a bagel. I was grateful to be living in an area where I could walk to almost all of the necessities. I was wearing my beeper hoping that Rodney would beep me. I had taken all the messages off the machine to make sure that if he called, there would be room for his message. I arrived at the apartment. Paula and Drew were just coming in from a party from the night before. He said he scored some fantastic weed and that I should join them in a morning cap. I laughed and agreed that I should join them for a morning cap. I forgot that I had to report to personnel on Wednesday, and they might take my blood. I walked into their den of smoke, rolling rock, and weed. I stayed there for the rest of the afternoon. It felt good being in a zombie state. I wouldn't have to think about the love I was about to lose. Finally, around 1700, I got up to go home. Paula and Drew were passed out. I bid them good evening and told them to lock the door. I don't think it ever got locked. I walked next door, placed my key in the door, opened it, locked it, and passed out on the couch. When I woke up it was Sunday. The apartment was about fifty degrees, and I had forgotten to turn on the heat. I immediately got up and turned on the heat, and put the coffee pot on. Realizing that I had no cream or food, I turned the coffee pot off. Putting on as many clothes as I could stand, I walked to the grocery store and bought the basics—eggs, cheese, milk, cream, bread, sausage, and a Sunday paper. It had gotten extremely cold outside but it felt good walking back to the apartment. Once again, as I entered the apartment, Paula and Drew were just coming in. I thought I had left them passed out. Paula said they got up around midnight and went to another party. I wondered if I wanted to continue where I left off yesterday. I declined and they just laughed.

I entered my apartment and finally looked around to see how dusty and dirty it was. It was time to do some housecleaning. I had no messages and my beeper had not gone off, so I should use my time productively. I placed Diane Ross's, "I'm coming out" album on the stereo, and went to work. Before I knew it, the apartment was clean and it was again around 1600. I thought this might be a great time to wash clothes so that is what I did. I gathered all the clothes I had from the safe house, and what I had left behind. I went to the piggy bank for quarters and looked under the sink for the detergent. I walked to the apartment complex laundry room. The two police officers that lived in the building were playing poker and waiting for their clothes. We greeted each other with the, "Where have you been?" and "We know you work for the secret service. Then we all laughed. I joined their poker game and there we all were until 2200 hours. At that point, one had a shift to take, the other was going to bed and I was not about to let them leave me down there alone. I had finished almost everything and what was not done could wait. I entered my apartment and once again, my body became extremely tired. This time, I did make it to the bedroom. I was able to set the clock, check the messages and my beeper. Nothing. I fell asleep thinking that I would never see Rodney again.

The next couple of days went along very uneventfully. Dr. Zarnoff wrote and I typed. I was still driving him back and forth to work, but if that is what I needed to do to keep a job, I was not about to complain. I was concerned because this was a temporary position. I asked Dr. Zarnoff if his assistant was coming back.

He said, "Why? Don't you like it here?"

I said, "Yes, but I understood this was a temporary position."

He replied, "I believe she has found another position, so you are here as long as you can stand me." Then he said, "Don't you have an appointment with personnel on Wednesday?"

I replied, "Yes."

He said, "Okay, they will take care of all the paperwork at that time."

I left his office thinking he knew more than he was letting on. Nevertheless, I didn't care. I enjoyed working for him, I was learning a great deal about radio waves, signals, and how they were going to be used in the future. One day, people would be listening to satellite radio, everyone would have cellular phones, and computers would be so small you'd be able to wear them on your wrist. I was not sure how all of that was supposed to happen, but it was great being part of the process.

Finally, on Tuesday night, I got a call from Rodney. He was leaving to go on a house hunting trip to California on Thursday and wondered if we could get together sometime on Wednesday.

I replied, "Great, I have to go to personnel on Wednesday, so why don't you meet me there? You can follow me to Virginia."

He replied, "Great, what time?"

I told him that I had to go to personnel at 1300 hours and I was sure it would not take more than an hour. I asked him to meet me there at 1430. He said he could make that happen. My heart came through my chest. I could hardly sleep. I needed someone to read me a bedtime story. I had to tell Dr. Zarnoff that he would be driving himself home on Wednesday. He would have to move his BMW. It was time for him to drive it. It had been at least a week.

I wanted to look extra special for Rodney. I had purchased a brown and black suede pantsuit from "Georgetown Leather Design" before we went on TDY and hadn't had a chance to wear it. I would wear my brown leather ankle boots and a black see-though blouse. That should make Rodney and Dr. Zarnoff happy. Even though he was gay, he would make remarks about women all the time. I wondered if he was bisexual, but we never spoke about the possibility. The night could not pass fast enough. I tossed and turned most of the night and was elated when the clock alarm went off at 0600. I showered slowly, put on his favorite perfume, and made sure it was all over my body. I curled my hair tightly so that it would last all day. I made sure my make-up was flawless and I was ready. Once at work, I reminded Dr. Zarnoff that I was leaving at noon in order to get to personnel by 1300. I asked Dr. Zarnoff what he wanted to eat and he told me he wanted his usual. I got his lunch, and cleared my area. My stomach was in a knot, not only because of Rodney, but also because of going to personnel.

I left at exactly 1200 and made it just in time. It had begun to snow a little and people in the district just couldn't handle snow. Once in the building, I pushed the button for the eleventh floor. The doors opened up to a well-decorated lobby, and there Rodney sat, looking like Godiva chocolate. We spoke and I continued through the double doors. I waited approximately ten minutes before the de-briefer arrived. We talked about forty-five minutes. He gave me papers to sign and that was it. There was no mention of the pictures. The de-briefer left and the personnel lady came in. She gave me additional papers to sign for my transfer into a new division. I didn't ask any questions. I signed the papers. The personnel person left the area, and then came back with copies for me.

She asked, "Do you have any questions?"

I politely replied, "No."

I was done with the entire procedure at approximately 1345. I left the area and went back through the double doors. Rodney was still waiting for me. As I walked through the area, he got up and followed me. We knew there would be no talking about the situation until we got into open air.

Once outside, we looked at each other and just shook our heads. The snow was falling harder and I knew it would take forever to get to Virginia. Even on a Wednesday, people with annual leave available would be leaving their jobs in record numbers just to get home in time for dinner. Rodney got into his vehicle and I got into mine. The minute we made it out to the main street, the traffic had backed up. We turned onto Independence Avenue to try to get to the Fourteenth Street Bridge. Somehow, Rodney had managed to let so many cars in, that he was about twenty cars behind me.

We inched on to the bridge, and I could not believe it had taken us an hour just to get there. By this time, the bridge had ice on it and people were sliding into the sides and tail spinning. I kept looking for Rodney in my rear view mirror, but I'd lost sight of him. We inched along another forty-five minutes. The weather had gone from bad to worse. The radio was reporting closures of businesses and roads. I could not wait to get off that bridge. I knew Rodney was behind me, but that would give me time to get into my apartment, shower, put a bottle of wine in the freezer, and prepare myself for a wonderful evening. As I slid off the bridge, I prayed I wouldn't hit a pole. The roads in Virginia had been plowed and were not as bad. I again looked in my rear view mirror. No sign of Rodney. I stopped at the light on Arlington Boulevard, hoping he would catch up. Then all of a sudden, a huge ball of fire and smoke came from the bridge.

A reporter interrupted a song on WHUR to report that, "A Boeing 737, two-engine jet airliner that was Air Florida Flight 90, descended and had taken a nose dive—high and tail low. At 4:01 p.m., the tail struck the deck and parapet of the Fourteenth Street Bridge. Additional details will be provided when we have more information. As of this moment, it is utter pandemonium. Back to our regularly scheduled programming."

Another one of Ila's diamonds was gone.

CPSIA information can be obtained at www.ICGtesting.com
Printed in the USA
LVOW08s0135180714

394761LV00001B/1/P